an anthology

DESIGNS by

Deliverance

and other stories

P. K. SMITHERMAN

Publishing Coordinator – Sharon Kizziah-Holmes

Paperback-Press
an imprint of A & S Publishing
Paperback Press, LLC
Springfield, Missouri

ISBN -13: 978-1-964559-73-5

DEDICATION

I dedicate this to my best friend, my brother Bob Lockhart. I still miss him every single minute, my world is darker without him in it.

CONTENTS

ACKNOWLEDGMENTS

I would be remiss if I did not acknowledge Debbie Otten. She has been a mentor, a stalwart support, an inspiration, and a true friend. Thank you Deb.

A LITTLE HELP FOR JANICE

———————◆◆◆———————

Richie had asked Janice for a date numerous times until finally Janice relented and agreed. Many girls were jealous because Richie was quite the lady's man, and he was considered a real man at almost twenty-one years old. He always had money. He always dressed nice. To parents, he gave the impression of a clean-cut young man/boy. This was his goal. He had his own house, he owned his own business, and appeared to have money to burn.

Richie was from New Jersey. His mom's sister lived here and she lost her husband three years ago. Richie's dad had also died. His aunt had been after her sister, Richie's mom, to move here for over two years until finally his mom relented and they moved here to stay with her. Richie was not yet nineteen but his dad had worked with his uncle so there were connections here for work. Richie had worked with his dad since he was fifteen so he was able to step right into the business and soon he owned his own travel agency. It was a proper travel agency that offered trips all over the world but they always had specials on trips to New Jersey and New York, and there was a little something extra going on in the back office. The travel agency took Richie out of town frequently.

When he met Janice's parents, he was the perfect gentleman. That was just the problem, he was a man. Well, maybe a man/boy, but almost five years older than sixteen-year-old Janice. Janice had warned them that he was a little older but this was clearly a lot older than they expected. They could appreciate that he appeared to be self-sufficient and certainly ambitious but he was too old for Janice. They were on the fence on whether they should allow this but the thing that swung the pendulum in his favor was the beautiful, intricate, gold crucifix he wore around his neck. Back in the sixties, it was not just a piece of jewelry, it meant a person believed in God.

Janice's parents did not give her their blessing on dating Richie, but they knew she was a good girl and trusted she would do the right thing.

Richie's friends were also impressive. They were all dapper, had nice homes, and spent a lot of money. One of Richie's colleagues had a younger sister, Maria, who went to school with Janice and her friends. That is how they all met. Janice and her friends loved going to Maria's house because it was like a mansion to them. Maria had a maid who was more than happy to serve the kids. They spend most of their time between the video arcade in the house and the outdoor, inground swimming pool. As it turned out, Maria's older brother and his friends were around a lot, as well.

There was also something very dangerous about Richie. He may have dressed as a gentleman but he was not always a gentleman. The other kids in Janice's group liked him for a variety of reasons. The boys liked him because he could always get alcohol. The girls liked him because they knew he was tough. He knew how to fight and evidently was very good at it. That was exciting to sixteen-year-old girls and boys.

For their date, Richie took Janice to the show. When he took her home, she kissed him at the door. A very small kiss. He was the perfect gentleman.

Her parents were still awake, it was 9:30pm, and witnessed Richie walking their daughter to the door. Her mom asked, "So how was the show, honey?"

"Oh it was great," said Janice, "I had a blast! Richie is amazing!"

"We kinda wanted to talk to you about that," said Mom. "I hope you know that we trust you. You've always been a smart girl but this is not a good match for you. He is too old. You need to be with kids your own age."

"But Mom," said Janice, "I really like him, and he really likes me. He treats me like a queen."

"I don't doubt that," answered Mom, "But after a while, he is going to get tired of hanging around with sixteen-year-old kids. You'll be okay with that so you will mostly be around his age group. That may sound enticing to you now but if that goes on, you will alienate all your friends and miss out on this best time of your life."

"I don't think that would happen. Those kids are my best friends," said Janice. "I am supposed to go to a party with him tomorrow. It's at his Boss's house, so some of his friends might be there but I don't think he would ever take me completely away from my friends."

"Think about it sweetheart, before you get in too deep," said Mom. "Also, you know you cannot be drinking alcohol, and I'm sure Richie's group will all be drinking. You are still five years away from that, don't forget it."

"Me and Richie have already talked about that, Mom," said Janice. "He admitted that his friends drink but honestly, I've not seen him ever take a drink. And he told me that even though he does drink on occasion, he does not want me to."

The next day Richie picked up Janice and they went to a party. Richie had told her that this was an important party. The host was his boss and very important to him. She took the hint that she should dress accordingly, so a little black dress and heels worked. She did not feel like a sixteen-year-old girl. She looked sophisticated. She felt sophisticated. He handed her a little jewelry box and told her there was only one thing missing. Inside was a beautiful gold, intricately sculpted, crucifix necklace. She opened it and let out a little squeal as she said, "Oh, God, it's beautiful Richie! It's just like yours only smaller."

He fastened it around her neck and said, "Now you are perfect."

The house was nothing short of a mansion with parking valets and servants. Richie was impressed by Janice's appearance and proud to introduce her as his girlfriend. With his arm around her waist, and being introduced as his girlfriend, Janice was in heaven. She could not believe the wealth around her. It was easy to see that everyone there had money. She was very impressed.

Janice was an intelligent sixteen-year-old girl but she was naive. There are many wealthy travel agency owners, but the people at this party did not make the majority of their money from travel agencies. This is what she believed though.

They had been there about an hour when Richie said, "Baby, I have to go meet with some of my associates. It shouldn't take long. There's lots of good eats around here if you're hungry. You can mingle with some of the other girlfriends. I'll be back as soon as I can." He kissed her, went into another room and closed the door. Janice wandered over to the buffet and started talking to some of the other girls. Most of the girls were friendly but there were a few that were definitely snobs.

About an hour later, the door opened and the men spilled out. Richie walked over to Janice, kissed her and told her they needed to leave. She was ready. They found the host, thanked him, said goodbye to a few others, then went out where the valet had their car ready. Janice noticed the hundred dollar bill that Richie discreetly handed to the valet. She thought how kind that was of Richie.

Once again, Janice's parents were awake when Richie walked Janice to the door. They watched as Richie gave her a kiss at the door. This one was a little longer than the first one they witnessed but they could tell that Janice was the one holding onto Richie.

Janice's parents never insinuated to her that Richie was involved in illegal activities but they were sure of it. Her parents were all legal now but back in their youth they were certainly not angels and they still had many connections. They knew about criminals and toughs, they grew up with them, they were them. Unbeknownst to Janice, anyone she had grown close to had been vetted. When she turned fifteen and began dating, those boys were secretly scrutinized even more.

Janice told them all about the party. It was obvious that she was very impressed. That did not set well with her parents. They did not like the fact that she was so impressed. Then again, she was a sixteen-year-old girl, and ultra impressionable. They were not sold on Richie at all and having to deal with her excitability was not a help. No matter how good he seemed to be with their daughter, she was still a little girl and not ready to be a woman. She needed to grow up with people her own age. It was not going to be easy getting her to quit Richie.

Janice was open to a discussion with her parents. They agreed that Richie was one heck of a guy and a real catch, for someone his own age. They pointed out the fact that she would be unable to grow up with people her own age since Richie and his friends were already grown. They reminded her of the sixteen-year-old things she loved to do that would no longer be done. What they did not mention was they were not naive and knew that his money did not come entirely from any travel agency. Janice listened to everything they had to say then went to her room.

The next day Janice told them that she would think about everything they told her and talk to Richie. The next few days were normal but when Saturday rolled around things got abnormal, fast. Richie came to pick up Janice and while she was still getting ready upstairs, he took the opportunity to talk with her parents alone.

"I know you don't want Janice going out with me," said

Richie. "It's too bad you don't like me because I have all the power, you see. I could take her completely away from you if I wanted, or I could just use her for a while then return her to you a little more experienced than when I first met her. It's just up to me now. I'm in control of that little girl so I need for you two to back the fuck off or you'll never see her again. Do we understand each other?"

Both parents nodded in response and said, "Yes."

"Okay, good," said Richie. "I'm going to be gone for a few days, heading to Miami on business, but we'll talk more when I get back."

Janice bounded down the stairs just in time to hear Richie say something about Miami. She asked, "Richie, are you going away again?"

"Yes," he answered, "but I shouldn't be gone very long. I'm leaving in a couple days but I'll call you as soon as I get back."

A week passed and Janice had not heard from Richie. After two weeks she had already left him three messages and his phone was still going directly to voice mail. After three weeks Janice was in tears and almost inconsolable. She had never become close with any of his friends, had never met his mom, and had never been to his travel agency. The only shared connection was Maria, her schoolmate. Maria told Janice that neither her brother, or any of his friends, had been able to reach Richie. They had no clue where he was or why he was gone so long.

Six weeks later and still no word. Janice's parents tried to console her as much as possible but now it was time for her to move on. To continue her normal life. Reconnect with her friends. She was heartbroken but she did try to resume life before Richie. Her parents were careful not to remind her that it was only nine weeks ago that she first met Richie, and merely three weeks of dating before he left. They wanted to shake her and tell her to get over it but they did not. They very diplomatically brought this into the conversation. What she may have thought was love was merely infatuation.

Janice turned back into the sparkly, happy, teenage girl she was before Richie entered her life. Her parents were happy too. Janice had two more years of exciting high school life before it was time for college. Richie's name had not surfaced for years.

Janice dated three different boys, all vetted of course, during her last years in high school but was single when she started at her prestigious, and very expensive, university. Even though she was an hour away at college her parents were not worried about it. Unknown to Janice, they had eyes everywhere. During her first year she dated only two young men. The first for about three months but the relationship with the second one was still ongoing when they went on summer break and Janice moved home. He did not live nearby so they got together on weekends so the parents were able to meet him in person.

They did not like him. His vetting proved questionable. He was a gold-digger. He was not at her college for education, in fact, he was not even in college. He saw dollar signs in Janice. Even his keychain was a tacky gold dollar sign. Alas, Janice was simply not a good judge of character. Once again, she had fallen for a real gem. During the summer break he came to visit Janice the first two weekends but then he stopped. Janice tried calling him when the third weekend went by and he did not show up. She left a message for him when it went to voice mail.

Two days later, Janice tried calling him again but this time there was an announcement that the number was discontinued. She was a little distraught but not too bad. Her parents told her that maybe the college proved to be too expensive and maybe his bills were catching up to him. Janice did not have his parents phone number or even his parents' names. She tried googling him and came up with nothing but that is not unusual so she tried googling students at the university and there was no such student. Her parents did not have to say a word to her, she volunteered it. She was almost taken in by a boy, again.

"How stupid can I be?" cried Janice. "Will I ever get smarter about boys?"

"Oh sweetheart, it's not your fault," her dad said.

Her mom looked at her and said, "Every time you get hurt, we get hurt right there with you honey. You're not stupid. You need to be strong and I don't know if it's true but you know that saying 'what doesn't kill you makes you stronger.' Maybe there is something to that. There should be a law that assholes have to wear a sign. Right now, just concentrate on school. When it's right, you'll know. You don't have to go looking for it."

After summer break Janice returned to school and concentrated on her education. She was doing great with her classes and looking forward to a career when she met someone, Tony. She was in her junior year and he was in med school. They met at a coffee shop. They talked for hours but they both admitted that they were dedicated to school at the time.

Over the rest of the semester they got together for coffee maybe once a week. Other than that they were all study. When summer break came they had both decided to continue to take classes so they only had a couple weeks for break. Janice went home for a week and Tony did the same. The next week they had a few real dates. They were both serious about their educations and swore they would not let a relationship interfere with their goals.

Janice told her parents about Tony and she also told them about their agreement to keep their relationship, but not at the cost of their goals. Because of all their coffee dates she could tell her parents a lot about this new young man. She told them he was going to medical school, his parents' names, his home town, where he went to high school and much more. Her parents thought this was a very good sign but they vetted him anyway and Tony passed with flying colors.

They were married when he was an intern at the

hospital near the university. He fell in love with Janice's home town, and her parents, so he arranged to practice medicine at the hospital there when he finished his internship. Her parents were ecstatic.

When the grandchildren started coming the grandparents were over the moon. They babysat their two grandchildren all the time. Their house was big and over the years they had remodeled almost every room in it. Her parents were big do-it-yourselfers.

Just before their fortieth anniversary, Janice's parents were killed in a car accident. Since her family had overgrown their house, they moved into her parents' house. Over the years her parents had remodeled so well that very little had to be changed. The only thing Janice wanted to change was the huge outdoor grill. It was an L shaped and all brick. It was beautiful but Janice decided they could remove one leg of the L shape to make more room on the patio. Demolition was easy for Tony. When it was finished he went inside the house and yelled out, "It's all done, hon, and it looks great!"

Janice looked out the back window and said, "Oh, it does! It looks so much bigger out there. We'll be able to fit more chairs out there now. You done good, sweetie! Thank you."

Tony reached in his pocket and pulled something out, "You need to see what I found in there. It's weird." He held out his hand and in it was a beautiful, intricate, gold crucifix necklace and a gold, dollar sign keychain.

DESIGNS BY DELIVERANCE

◆◆◆

Part 1

She learned to sew before she was seven years old. Her papa was a coal miner and her mama mended clothes for the miners that did not have a woman to do it for them. The mending business grew so much that her papa and mama saved up so they could buy a sewing machine. The sewing machine cost $33 in 1930 but it turned out to be the best $33 ever spent. Mama quickly taught herself how to sew on the new machine and her business doubled or tripled within a couple of weeks. So much so, that she taught her six-year-old daughter, Deliverance, how to use the machine as well. Pretty soon the machine was going non-stop for sixteen hours a day, or more, and the finished products were usually better than brand new. Although they charged only pennies for mending, their investment paid for itself within weeks.

Deliverance fell in love with the machine. Her skill for sewing surpassed her mama's by the time she was ten years old. Even her mama recognized her gift for sewing. It was not long before she was creating clothes out of any material they could afford and then using the scraps for new creations. The little general store in the village offered to help Deliverance with her product and for a small commission, would put them on display for sale.

Things were finally looking up for the family when a

year later her papa was killed in a mine explosion. Deliverance was eleven years old. She and her mama had to take in more mending to pay the bills, but it was no longer fun for Deliverance like it had been before. Now it was just work. She no longer enjoyed just being at the sewing machine and creating new things.

Life went on. Deliverance married a local man and had a son and a daughter. The daughter married and moved away but the son, Jerome, stayed in the area. Jerome married and had two sons but while the sons were still young, Jerome and his wife succumbed to a virus and they both died. The sons remained with their grandmother.

After they had graduated from school, one of the grandsons married and moved away but the other grandson, Jess, stayed and remained very close to his grandmother, Deliverance. When he married, his wife, Jean, became close to his grandmother too and when they had a daughter, they named her Deliverance. They called her Livvy. Deliverance was seventy-two years old when Livvy was born but this little girl brought back the younger girl in Deliverance too.

Deliverance babysat Livvy, so they spent almost every day together. One of Livvy's first words was "Grey," which was short for Great Grandma. That was a mouthful for a toddler so Livvy would clumsily say "Grey Gramma", but she just took it upon herself to shorten it to Grey, and it stuck. Soon her mom and dad were also calling her Grey.

Although Livvy was only a child, she and her grandmother would sit and talk for hours. There was no seventy-two year age difference here, there was a special bond. Deliverance loved her great granddaughter like there was no tomorrow. She knew this little girl was special and for the first time in over fifty years she felt like she wanted to make something for someone. For Livvy. Deliverance went to the basement and dug out the old long forgotten sewing machine. She cleaned it and took it back to the sewing room and tested out the old treadle machine for the first time in many years. She still had material in her old sewing chest, so she started sewing. She did not use patterns, everything she created was original. The first finished product was a beautiful dress for Livvy.

Part 2

At six years old, Livvy became a celebrity of sorts because of her clothes. Not just with her classmates, but with their mom's as well. These clothes were stunning. When Livvy's parents were confronted about this, they had to give all the credit to Livvy's great grandmother, Deliverance, who at seventy-eight years old was sewing original clothes.

Within a few months, word had spread about the six-year-old's great grandmother, Deliverance, the seamstress. Parents at the school were asking if they could order clothes for their kids. When Deliverance was approached about this, she got excited and felt alive again. She was happy to do this. The customers would buy the materials and because Deliverance enjoyed it so much, she had no idea what to charge. This was bringing her joy. She left it up to the customer to 'donate' what he or she felt it was worth.

One day, one of the parents approached Deliverance and said, "Miss Deliverance, my name is Angela. I work at a marketing firm and would very much like to talk to you about your abilities."

Deliverance was still sharp as a tack as she looked at Angela and asked, "What exactly do you mean, my abilities?"

"It's more like magic, I admit," responded Angela. "I have seen your clothes. Every dress, shirt, skirt, blouse and pants have been original. No two are ever alike. Maybe it's a subtle change but they are all different and the way they are made, well, it's obvious they are of top-notch quality. I would love to help you market your products."

"You mean like hang a sign outside and sell my stuff?" asked Deliverance.

"Oh no. Nothing like that. These are too extraordinary for something as simple as that," replied Angela. "These days there are still walk-in stores, but the easiest and fastest way to reach people is online. Please tell me you will at least let me prepare something to present to you."

"Let me talk this over with my grandson and his wife," said Deliverance.

"Yes, please, they should be included too." Angela took out a card, handed it to Deliverance and said, "Give me a call when you have talked it over with them, please. Anytime."

This was the beginning of the enterprise called *Designs by Deliverance.*

Deliverance's house was big, so her grandson, Jess, and his family moved in so they could help. Livvy already spent a few days a week with her great grandmother, but this meant all day and night, every day and night, and she was ecstatic. Jess did the needed repairs and upgrades to the house to accommodate the family.

It was on Livvy's 10th birthday when she asked her great grandmother if she could try the machine. She had been watching Deliverance sew for years and she just knew she would be able to do it too. She had watched how her great grandmother had put her forehead on the machine before she started sewing so she did the same. When nothing happened, she asked Deliverance, "Grey, why do you put your head on the machine?"

"That's when the machine talks to me, Sweetie," answered Deliverance.

"What does it say?" asked Livvy.

"I'm not sure, Honey, maybe it just tells me what it's going to create next so I can help with the material it needs," answered Deliverance. "I think the machine is the brains of the operation. It thinks up new designs and we give that to the company to duplicate. They have other people that copy what the machine created, and people seem to want to buy these designs. Years ago, when we first got the machine, it didn't start talking to me right away but when it did, things got more interesting, and the work seemed to sew itself. My mama noticed that."

Livvy put her forehead to the arm of the machine again, squinched up her face like she was trying hard to get something and said, "It's not talking to me. Why isn't it talking to me?"

"Maybe it's not ready to talk to you yet. Give it time," said Deliverance.

Part 3

Deliverance was eighty-nine years old when she got sick. *Designs by Deliverance* had grown into a booming business with her grandson, Jess, his wife, Jean, and of course Livvy at the helm. At seventeen years old, Livvy could sew better than a lot of seamstresses, but she still did not have the magic touch of her great grandmother. Over the years she had witnessed the magic that was created by Deliverance. Her great grandmother had always said it came from the sewing machine, but Livvy never thought it was the machine at all, the magic was Deliverance. Every time she expressed this though, Deliverance told her it was the machine. She also told her to be patient because she felt it was going to talk to her soon, just like it did with her. On more than one occasion Deliverance told Livvy, "When it starts talking to you, and I think it will soon, just feed the feed dog. Give it what it wants and don't get in its way. I've always been very respectful of the feed dog and the presser foot. Just feed it like it asks and it will give you beautiful things. It pulls magic from you darlin, it makes sense after you see what it does. And don't be scared, it will never hurt you."

"Grey, when you leave me, I think the machine will go into the basement again and there will be no more *Designs by Deliverance*," sobbed Livvy. "You are Deliverance, and these are your designs. I don't want to even think about doing this without you."

Deliverance looked at Livvy and said, "Oh sweetie. Remember, you are Deliverance too. I want you to continue this. I know, I know for sure now, that the machine will talk to you. Maybe it's just waiting for me to be gone. Maybe the machine just works with one Deliverance at a time." Tears slid out of Deliverance's eyes as she told Livvy, "There's something that I've never told you. I've never told anyone. It still makes me cry to think about it, but I have to tell you. It happened when I was a young girl, much younger than you, not long after the machine started talking to me."

"You know I love you forever and always," Livvy choked out, "You can tell me anything."

Livvy fluffed some pillows so Deliverance could sit up a little straighter in bed as she started her regretful story. Deliverance took a deep breath and let out a bigger sigh as she started, "It was hot and we had no air conditioning back then, so we left the doors open. One day a little possum wandered into the house. You know me, I wouldn't kill any animal. Never. Not in a million years and I know you're the same. Well, he was wandering around the sewing room when I first caught sight of him. I started to talk really soft, so as not to scare him but it still did a little. He jumped up on the table with the machine and as I walked over to get him, his foot hit the feed dog and the presser foot went down on his little paw. It was hurting him, and I was running by then to get him and set him free, but it was too late. I closed my eyes and screamed. I know he screamed, and I know to me it sounded like it went on forever in my head, but I know for a fact that it was only a matter of seconds because when I stopped screaming and opened my eyes, he was gone. There was no sign of him anywhere. No blood. No bones. No hair. No trace. Except one. On the table was the cutest little muff I had ever seen." Livvy looked at Deliverance quizzically and her grandmother added, "Girls used to carry muffs to keep their hands warm. Anyway, this was the same color as the possum. It was beautiful. The fur was perfect and there was no trace of blood or smell or anything bad."

"After that," Deliverance whispered "I put my forehead on the arm of the machine, like I usually do, but this time I was crying. The craziest thing happened. It felt like the machine was crying with me. I could feel it was hurting, just like me. It knew that made me sad and it was sorry. I'm telling you the machine cares about me, and I care about it. This is what's going to happen to you too. You're the next Deliverance. The machine can't live without us. It cares about us. From then on, I never had to worry about animals around it. I knew they were safe. You know your dog and cat have been around it. Your cat curls around it. I think it kind of talks to them too, now. I think it feels protective. They feel that, and they feel safe now around it. People though, people aren't innocent like animals. I don't think it would do anything to other people though, unless it felt they meant harm to us. I don't know though. Over the years, the only thing I do know for sure is that it loves me, it cares about me, it missed me while I was gone for all those years. Found out I missed it too. I've known since then that it would never hurt me, and now I know it will never hurt you either. You're the next Deliverance. It will work for you, same as it did for me."

"Oh, Grey, why would you keep this sad thing to yourself for so many years? I'm so sorry. I know that broke your heart, but you know you could always tell me anything," said Livvy with tears running down her cheeks now too.

"I didn't think it was time and I knew you were the only one who would believe me. That's because you're the one who will take over. I know that now." Deliverance said quietly. "I knew, or at least hoped, that you would continue and be the next Deliverance in *Designs by Deliverance*. That's why I wanted you to know about the machine. Tell me you won't let the machine die." Deliverance wiped her tears, sighed deep and said to Livvy, "I'm tired now darlin,

I need to sleep, and you need to think about everything. Come back to talk more later. I love you forever and always."

Livvy helped Deliverance get comfortable, kissed her forehead, and as she walked out of the room she said, "I'll be back later Grey, I love you."

Part 4

Deliverance passed away quietly during her sleep with her family by her side. It was on her ninetieth birthday. Livvy was eighteen years old, and her grief was beyond compare.

Even though they lived in a small community more than a hundred people attended the funeral. Outside of Livvy and her parents, the only other relation was her uncle. She did not know him well, he only visited once a year. The only thing she knew about him was that he divorced his wife a couple years back and her dad tried to talk him into moving back home, so he could be with family. Her dad, Jess, was happy to see his brother, Jerry, again but was surprised when he came home with a new wife and a nineteen-year-old stepdaughter, Madison.

After the funeral there were dozens of people at the house, and they all had good things to say about Deliverance. It was nice, but very sad, at the same time. It was a very hard time for Livvy. She had lost her great grandmother, her mentor, her teacher, and her best friend. She was sitting on a window bench silently thinking of her loss when her uncle Jerry's stepdaughter approached. She looked at Livvy and said, "Hey, sorry about your loss."

"Thanks Madison," answered Livvy. "I really don't feel like talking right now, so excuse me." She got up and started walking away.

Madison called after her, "Sure, we can talk later."

Livvy went into the sewing room and closed the door. Her dad saw her leave and followed. He walked in and they both started crying. "Dad, what are we going to do without

Grey?" Livvy sobbed.

"We're going to do what she wanted us to do, we're going to carry on," replied her dad. "We know it won't be the same, but she knows how much we loved her, she knew we would be sad, but she wanted us to be happy. And family. She wanted us to carry on with the family and her business so that's what we'll do." They hugged again and as he walked toward the door he turned and said, "I have to go back out, there's a lot of people here. You can stay in here if you need to be alone. Do you want me to close the door?" Livvy nodded.

She could not stop the tears. She walked over to the sewing machine and sat down. She pictured Grey sitting there for hours, and she rested her forehead on the machine like she had seen her grandmother do so many times. With tears running down her face she said in a whispered voice, "Do you miss her too?" Suddenly, a strong tingling went through her entire body, like a bolt of lightning, but not painful at all, in fact it felt good, kind of familiar and comforting. Livvy felt something more too, it was like something was sharing her pain and loneliness. It helped. All kinds of feelings went through her as she realized the machine was talking to her, just like Grey had said it would. Then, while her forehead was on the arm of the machine and her tears were dropping on the bedplate something else happened. It was like a dream, but she was fully awake. She saw visions of a young girl at the machine quickly grow into an older woman, many visions of the past, but not her past. She knew she was seeing Grey's life through the machine. This wonderful machine was grieving for Grey and somehow the shared grief between the two of them made it a little easier. Just like her grandmother had always told her about grief being like a pie. She said that if several people had a slice, it made it a little easier. She knew that the machine had a very big slice of grief. She felt it.

Livvy's feelings were torn. She was mourning her grandmother, of course, but also excited about the machine. She had not planned on working the machine anymore, in fact, she had not planned on ever looking at it again. It was just too painful. Now that she felt the connection though, and the machine's grief, she knew what her grandmother had been talking about for all these years. She walked over to the couch and laid down as her cat went over to the machine and curled around it. She wondered if her cat was comforting the machine or vice versa, or both.

Part 5

Livvy's dad Jess, although torn up at the loss of his grandmother, was happy to see his brother, Jerry. Jerry had been on the West Coast nearly all of his adult life and Jess missed him. Jerry was an electrician by trade but when jobs got a little tight, he became what would be called a self-taught handyman. He was efficient at carpentry, plumbing, and of course electrical issues. He had even learned some landscaping.

They had arrived on Deliverance's last day, so she was able to see her other grandson before she passed. She had raised her grandsons together and was happy to see them that way again. Jess had insisted that they stay at the house during their visit.

After the funeral the two brothers were able to reconnect. They caught each other up with their lives. Jerry told Jess that he was afraid that he may have made a big mistake on his marriage. They had only known each other for four months. He told him about how they met and how he believes now it was a big mistake. He wanted his brother's input on this.

Jess looked at him and told him, "You're my brother, you know you can tell me anything."

Jerry looked embarrassed as he began his story. He said, "The company where I worked as an electrician went out of business, so I was reduced to handyman jobs. Fortunately, at least at first, there was a lot of demand for little jobs like painting, carpentry, maybe a little plumbing, so I was happy to get these. Most of these jobs lasted from three days to a week, and for a while, I was even booked months in advance. Every day when I finished, I would stop by this little diner close to home. I was a regular. You know I'm a friendly guy so when the new waitress, Patty, started working there, we would talk every day. Looking back now I see some red flags I should have caught then. I feel stupid."

"Jerry, there's nothing that can't be fixed," said Jess, "Whatever it is we can fix this, we can get through it together."

"Thanks," said Jerry, "You don't know how good I feel being home." Jerry looked at his brother with moist eyes. "It hurts, but I don't know if Patty really loves me. I think she may just be doing her stupid daughter's bidding."

"What happened?" asked Jess.

Jerry looked down at his lap and back up and said, "Like I said, we started talking every day, just like I did with all the regulars and employees there. Patty and I started dating and one day I complimented her on the beautiful blouse she was wearing. She kind of blushed and said she was guilty of borrowing it, it was her daughter's. She told me it was by a company that her daughter raved about called *Designs by Deliverance*. I couldn't help myself. I bragged that Deliverance was in fact, my grandmother. After all, I am terribly proud of our grandmother doing that. I know you guys played a huge part in the success of the company and I felt a little sad, and maybe even a little envious, that I was not a part of it. My bragging did not have that much of an impact on her, but she was terribly anxious to tell her daughter, Madison. I met Madison that very night, before our date. She normally made a point of being gone when I was at their apartment but this time, she made sure she was present. She was so present that night that she insisted we all stay home and order in so she could get to know me better. She was only interested in our grandmother.

Looking back, I see that quite clearly now."

Jess could see the hurt in his brother, now his eyes were moist when he said, "I'm so sorry, but I'm glad you're home now. You know you have a lot of love here."

"Anyway," Jerry continued, "Madison was asking me all about my family and it seemed to me, at the time, that she was genuinely interested in me, and happy that I was with her mom. That night Patty barely spoke a word. It was almost as if I was on a date with Madison. At one point her mom even told her to leave me alone for a while but she was relentless. I think she saw dollar signs, even though I told her I had nothing to do with the business. Nonetheless, she was dead set on learning all she could about it. I think it was then that she decided she would have to be in the family one way or another. I should have seen her for the loser she is right then. I knew her mom had told me she could not keep a job, or at least did not want to keep a job. Patty held two jobs while Madison would not even keep one."

"From that point on, Madison basically threw her mom at me. She would get me aside and tell me how much her mom looked forward to seeing me every day, how happy her mom was since I was in her life, how much her mom loved me, and all this crap that I should have known was bullshit but I was so lonely. Madison knew that and the little bitch knew how to play me. It worked. I told her on more than one occasion that I was never involved with the business, but she just kept on with the lies anyway. Thinking back now, I wish I had confronted her mom now with all this shit. Used my head a little more instead of my stupid lonely heart. I think I got played, but the worst part is that I still haven't confronted Patty about how she really feels about me. I know we're married so you must think I'm a real idiot, but everything was just so quick."

Jess looked at Jerry and asked him, "Do you love Patty?"

Jerry answered, "Yes, but I can't stand her daughter and I'm not so sure that Patty is crazy about her either. She knows how she uses her. She's mean to her too, but Patty is so afraid that she isn't a good Mom that she gives in to her and lets her treat her like shit. Madison even makes her feel bad about being raised by a single Mom, but get this, she's a widow! Patty's husband was killed in a car accident when Madison was young. Madison is a horrible person. I feel terrible for saying that, but she is evil. I'm sorry I brought her into this house."

"Oh shit," said Jess. "Okay, first thing you need to do is get straight with Patty. Take her on a walk out in the woods where you can be alone and see how you two really feel about each other. Get your relationship sorted. Madison is nineteen so she won't be around much longer. She even mentioned that she can't wait to get back to the west coast. She is just hanging around here to see what she can get. When she finds out she won't be seeing anything from the business she'll pack her bags and head back. You need to stay here with family. Patty too, if that's what you want. Above all, don't worry that you brought evil into this house. We may not look it, but we are equipped to handle it."

The brothers hugged, a good long hug, reassurance of love. Jess told Jerry again how much he had missed him and then he said, "Jerry, I would like it if you would stay here."

Part 6

The week following the death of Deliverance was a blur for the family. Jess was able to talk Jerry and his family into staying for a while, but Jess insisted on doing repairs needed to the house in exchange. The manager of the company that duplicated the new Deliverance fashions was more than patient. They still had an abundance of clothing designs delivered that they had yet to clone and send out to stores and warehouses, so they did not bother the family during this uncertain time. The only thing that they did ask was whether *Designs by Deliverance* was still in business.

Livvy was left in charge of this and after her talks with the machine she assured them the business was still intact. Her parents had been concerned about this. They never understood the relationship Grey had with the sewing machine; they thought the magic was Grey. This was true and nobody knew this as much as Livvy, but, she had since connected with the machine and knew the machine was magic, as well. The magic was shared now with the new Deliverance, Livvy. She told her parents about the connection she now shared with the machine and while they were happy that Livvy wanted to continue, they were not one hundred per cent sure the company could withstand the death of Deliverance. They would soon find out that this was not a concern.

A few weeks had gone by, and Livvy was as busy with new fashions as her great grandmother had been. Her parents saw right away that *Designs by Deliverance* was still very much in business and growing bigger. All the business details were left to them so they were happy to know that they would not be looking for other jobs anytime soon. In fact, the business was doing so well that they found they needed additional help, so Jess offered permanent positions to both Jerry and Patty. Jerry had been working on the house for three weeks straight and because of this, the old house was now better than ever. He had upgraded the plumbing and electricity on the third floor so that now there was so much livable space that Jess invited his brother and sister-in-law to move in. The house was huge and now every room in it was livable thanks to Jerry. Jerry planned more renovations but never to take away the integrity of the beautiful Victorian house, only to refurbish it to its original state.

For a little celebration, Jess, Jean, Jerry, and Patty went out to dinner. Livvy was invited but politely declined, telling them to have a good time. She did not know it at the time, but Madison had also declined the invitation.

Livvy, usually the cat and sometimes the dog, spent a

great deal of time in the sewing room so that is where she went. This night it was her and the cat. Livvy went over to the old chest where Grey had put material scraps and other things she could not throw away. She started looking through it, gently moving the contents around, when she ran across the most beautiful dark grey object. She picked it up, looked it over carefully, then burst into tears when she realized what it was. It was a beautiful muff. It was the opossum. Her great grandmother had kept it all these years, yet it broke her heart every time she even thought about it. Of course, Livvy was the only one in the world that knew the story and it was a story that would die with her. Just as all these sad thoughts were going through Livvy's mind, the door opened and in stood Madison.

"Hi cuz!" said Madison. "Don't you think it's about time you and me had a talk?"

"First," replied Livvy, "we are not really cousins so if you don't mind, please call me Livvy. Second, it sounds like you have some particular 'talk' in mind. What would that be?"

Madison smirked a little and said, "Well, Livvy, everybody else has a part of this company. I want a part too."

Livvy stood up, closed the chest and said, "So you want a job?"

"No, I don't want a job, you stupid cow," Madison giggled a little as she said that. "I just want a part of this company too. I'm family so I'm entitled."

"You are not family, you are not entitled, and I believe you're drunk," said Livvy.

"I've seen you rest your head on this stupid sewing machine, and then start sewing a new outfit," she said a little loud and then a little louder still, "So what is it with this thing? It's an old, antique, sewing machine. So, is it magic or something? Do you talk to it? I think you need to tell me more right now."

"You need to leave right now. Go back to the west coast

where you belong. You are not allowed in this room anymore," said Livvy with conviction.

"I am going back home, but not to the apartment we used to live in. I'm going back with money, so I don't need this anymore." She pulled a taser from her back pocket and held it in front of Livvy.

The cat was curled around the machine but stood, arched its back, and hissed as Madison walked over to the machine. "I've already told my mom goodbye, that I was leaving today, so I need you to give me some money right now or I'm going to destroy this stupid machine. What's in that chest? Is there money in there?"

"I don't have any money, you cow, and get away from me with that taser and get away from the machine!" yelled Livvy.

Livvy stood in front of the machine, guarding it from Madison. The cat continued to hiss at Madison, ready to pounce. Madison turned on the taser and Livvy could see the blue streaks of lightning pulsing between the two points on the stun gun. Several things happened at once then. As Madison lunged toward Livvy with the activated taser, the protective cat jumped on her shoulder and starting clawing at her. Livvy grabbed the arm with the stun gun and as Madison whirled around her free hand rested on the bed of the sewing machine and lightly touched the feed dog. The sewing machine started itself, the presser foot lowered and the feed dog started feeding Madison's hand into the machine.

As quickly as all hell had broken loose, it was done. The cat was once again curled around the quiet machine. There was absolutely no trace of Madison except a brand new, gorgeous little denim jacket on the bed of the sewing machine. Embroidered on each tip of the collar were very intricate miniature stun guns, with beautiful, bright, blue electric streaks passing between the taser points. Livvy knew right away that this was going to be a big fashion hit.

A SIMPLE PROCEDURE

◆ ◆ ◆

Anyone who has ever been on blood thinners will agree that it is a royal pain in the ass, and once they have been prescribed, it takes practically an act of congress to get off the medication. Gabby's cardiologist told her that when a cardiologist puts someone on medication, they are generally on it for life.

A patient on blood thinners needs to go to a clinic every week, or if lucky, every two weeks, to get their fingers pricked and blood tested. This tells them whether the dose should be lowered or raised. It is a hassle.

Gabby had been on blood thinners for over three years and the doctors were all very pleased with her heart function so she asked to be taken off this medication. She had no idea it would be so difficult. She had two choices. The first choice was to go on a medication that would not require weekly blood testing but this was not covered by her insurance and would have been hundreds of dollars a month so that choice was abandoned immediately. The second choice would be a process lasting three to five years but during that time she would be off medication. It was a loop recorder implant.

The loop recorder device measures two inches long and one-half inch wide and is implanted under the skin near the heart. This device is tied to a cell phone that records and monitors and is devoted only to the loop recorder. It must be plugged in at all times and be within six feet of the bed. These implants normally remain with a person for three to five years, or even longer.

All this just to go off a medication. Ridiculous, huh?

So, Gabby chose the loop recorder and after over two years, and no noticeable heart problems, she wanted it removed. She was surprised, but happy when her cardiologist agreed to the removal.

This removal process requires that the device be removed via the same incision in which it was first implanted. Simple and straight-forward. Wait a minute. One catch. The device has moved around a bit and the surrounding body has attached itself. Ouch.

As with any procedure performed in a hospital, a person has to jump through many hoops of all sizes and shapes.

The morning of the procedure Gabby's alarm sounded at 4:30am. They were supposed to be at the hospital at 5:30am. The actual surgery was not scheduled until 7:30am but the patient is always required to wait around for at least two hours.

Gabby and Hayes, her husband, were at the hospital by 5:30am as ordered. They went through registration, usual questions by a nurse, and a signature. For this they had to be there two hours before the procedure. They were taken to a hospital room, and Gabby changed into a hospital gown. She was able to keep her underwear on and instead of their ugly socks, she chose to keep her own footies. This later proved to be a mistake. Nurses are in and out for about thirty minutes, each asking the same questions as the one before. Now they wait.

Gabby turned on the TV and they watched two entire episodes of Green Acres with no word from the doctor yet. Finally, feeling the result of getting up that early, and not sleeping well, Gabby told Hayes she was going to try to shut her eyes for a minute. Of course, this prompted the arrival of an orderly with a gurney.

She transferred over to the gurney and they headed out of the room and down the hall. The orderly had asked for her birthday, as is the rule, to make sure he had the right patient. Any time spent in the hospital is one where you are repeating your birthday dozens of times. As he rolled her down the hallway, he looked at her papers and said, "So, you're getting knee surgery today, huh? Bet you'll be glad when that's done."

"Wait, what?" asked Gabby. "No, no, that's not what I'm here for! Turn around, I'm not here for knee surgery! Turn around! Take me back to the room." The orderly looked shocked at how excited she got. He stopped the gurney and tried to calm her down. She jumped off the gurney.

He said, "Stop, don't worry, we'll get to the bottom of this. I just have the wrong papers. It's not a big deal.

"It is a big deal, you idiot!" she said. "How can you say it's not a big deal? I'm in here for what's supposed to be a very simple procedure and you're trying to get me to knee surgery. That's a big deal to me!"

"I get it, I get it, I'm sorry," he said. "Get back up on the gurney and I'll take you back to your room then I'll go to the nurse's station and get this straightened out."

"I'm not getting back on there," she said, "I'll get back to my room myself." She started walking back down the hall and he started following her.

He got close to her and said, "Hey please get back on the gurney or I'll get in trouble. You're not supposed to be walking around." He was practically beside her then so she took off running down the hall. As she tried to round the corner, her footies, unable to gain purchase, slid on the perpetually waxed hospital floor. She ran into another orderly, bounced off of him and was thrown down. There was an echoing thud as her head met the floor. There was blood. She was unconscious.

The orderlies looked at each other while one said, "Hurry up, we got to get her on the gurney and to the ER!" They retrieved her and raced to the emergency room. They explained what happened to the attending doctor as she examined Gabby's head.

"She's gonna need stitches so grab a nurse to get her prepped," said the doctor.

Gabby regains consciousness as a nurse is shaving a spot on Gabby's head. "What the hell is going on?" She tries to get up but realizes she is strapped to a gurney. "I'm gonna scream if someone doesn't explain this real quick!"

The nurse tries to calm her down as she explains how she got to this point. "You hit your head quite hard when you fell. How are you feeling?"

Gabby was still dazed as she answered, "My head hurts, but I guess you knew that."

"Yes, I'm sorry," said the nurse. "I believe the doctor is also going to want to get an MRI just to be on the safe side."

"You mean it could be a skull fracture?" Gabby asked.

"That is a possibility," said the nurse.

"What do you do for that? You're not talking about surgery or anything for that, are you? I can go home, right?" asked Gabby

The nurse looked at Gabby and said, "First of all, it might not be fractured at all, most likely it isn't. The doctor just wants to make sure. If it is fractured, she would probably want you to stay in the hospital for a little while, maybe a day or two, to make sure you are properly monitored."

"An MRI?" asked Gabby. "Jesus! I came in here for a supposedly simple procedure and now I'm going for an MRI? Can someone please tell my husband what's going on?"

The words had barely escaped her mouth before she saw Hayes standing beside her. He was asking her something but it took a second for her to realize what he was asking her. "Gabby, they're here for you. You need to go."

She sat straight up, looked at Hayes, then at the orderly at the door and realized she had fallen asleep. "What a nightmare!"

She said hello to the orderly and of course gave him her birthday and they were on their way. As he rolled her down the hallway, he looked at her papers and said, "So, you're getting knee surgery today, huh? Bet you'll be glad when that's done."

Avery's Garden

---◆◆◆---

Part 1

Avery was told that this 'fresh start' was mostly for her. She did not need a fresh start; she just needed her dad to see the real person he had married. She felt discouraged that a fresh start was not going to change that. Her dad was determined to make it work though, so there they were, at the newest fresh start. This time it meant moving to a very rural part of the state. According to her dad, it was somewhere that they could decompress from city life. A place where his eleven-year-old daughter could commune with nature. He knew she loved that.

The fresh start was not entirely about her. It might be for her stepmother's roving eye. They did not think Avery knew anything. They thought she was too young to know about these things. She knew though. She knew how easily her stepmother made new friends and, in the city, there was a new friend around every corner. She tried to tell her dad once that she did not trust his new wife but that did not end well so she never mentioned it again. She missed her mom, and she knew that her dad did as well.

This fresh start was far enough out where each house sat on no less than three acres. Everyone had their own well and septic system, the only thing that connected them to town was electricity. Neighbors were still close but not so close you could spit and hit their house. It was nice. Avery liked it. The house was big so that was another plus for Avery. She could have some alone time. It was a two-story house with the master bedroom and a big office for her dad, Dave, downstairs so Avery figured she could stay upstairs to cut down on interaction with her stepmother, Marisa.

The previous owners had made a vegetable garden at the back of the house so planting anything would be easy. In the front there were flowers across the entire house and two other flower gardens in the front, one on each side of the driveway. They were each surrounded by beautiful landscape rocks in the shape of a circle surrounding a tree in the center. The flowers inside were lush. There was no room for any possible additions. They were beautiful. The previous owners had certainly taken time to make these wonderful show pieces. You could tell that they loved this house. They were both elderly and had been there for many years.

Mr. and Mrs. Huggins. They had lived on this land for thirty years. The original house had been remodeled twice during their time there. They had a son and a daughter but they both lived quite a distance from them, so visits were limited to birthdays and holidays. Neither had children so there were no grandchildren to tear up Mrs. Huggins' beautiful flowerbeds. Avery thought of them as a cuddly old couple. She felt that even the name, Huggins, was endearing.

Evidently, Mrs. Huggins had a heart attack while she was out in the very back of the property. She died instantly. When Mr. Huggins could not find her he ventured to the back property where she had just recently started visiting. He found her. His stroke was not fatal but left him, at least temporarily, unable to take care of himself. The children were summoned, but since they were anxious to get back home, they agreed to take him home with them and find him an assisted living property nearby so their need to sell the property was urgent.

Avery could not help but feel sorry for the elder Huggins couple and a little sad that she was so happy to be living in their home now. It was especially sad that Mrs. Huggins died in the space that Avery loved so much. The back part of the property was like heaven and Avery learned that Mrs. Huggins had only recently started visiting the back area. She wondered why the couple had not visited the back part of their property more. It was about two acres of total beauty back there, and all to Avery.

Avery's dad, Dave, had created an on-line security program that had almost immediately become extremely popular and very lucrative. He had an office in the city that was always manned, but most of his time was spent working from home. Especially now that he had the ultimate home office with a view of the woods right outside his window. He did make a point of going into the office at least once a week, and sometimes more. He wanted to believe that his staff was trustworthy, but he had to make sure that they were not just working hard on the days that he was present. He would make surprise visits and was more than satisfied when he learned that his staff was indeed working when he was not there. Now he was comfortable working from home most days.

Avery's stepmother did not want to move to the 'boonies' as she called it but she knew that her husband would go without her so she could not let go of the easy life she had with him. At least not yet. She knew she was walking on thin ice with Dave, and she had to watch her step. She knew that Dave did not trust her after he had caught her on more than one occasion whispering and flirting a little too much for a married woman. He had not caught her acting on anything yet, and thankfully for her, he had not diligently investigated some of her whereabouts. She was lucky so far, but it was only a matter of time before she was bored enough to go looking for trouble. Avery did not trust her and was worried that her dad would get hurt. When her mom died, she knew the hurt her dad felt because she also suffered. She was six years old, and they tried to console each other but it was so devastating to both that it was of little help. Time was the only healer. She was happy when her dad met Marisa and she could see a little part of him come alive again. Avery was not going to let the fact that she did not trust Marisa interfere with any happiness it may bring her dad.

Part 2

Avery finished sixth grade at her old school. She was eleven years old, four feet, nine inches tall. It appeared she was going to take after her father, tall and lean. As a tween she had just started her growth spurt and by the end of the summer she would most likely be an additional three inches taller. With that growth spurt and a birthday two months away, Avery would be starting seventh grade at twelve years old and probably over five feet tall. So, with seventh grade three months away Avery had time on her hands to start exploring her new backyard. She loved that there was a little wooded area full of mature trees beyond the back yard. That is where she started her property investigation. She loved that most of the trees back there were too big for her to get her arms around. She was a tree hugger. She loved the smell of the bark and the rough feel of it on her skin. Her dad would just smile when he saw Avery go to every tree and give it a big hug. He was a bit of a tree hugger himself; he was just not as demonstrative as his daughter.

Avery was what used to be called a tomboy. Today both girls and boys are usually so wrapped up in their smart phones, computers, and electronic games that they do not even want to commune with nature, to take an interest in trees or bugs. In fact, it is rare to see kids playing outside anymore. A few years ago, you could see kids playing catch or playing hide and seek but today they seem to be more wrapped up in their technical gadgets. It would appear that the recent generations had foregone what would have been considered physical exercise for more sophisticated pastimes. Their computers offered every kind of game, hence no need to go outside.

Avery was different in that sense. She preferred being outside even though she had her own phone and a computer. She was a tweenaged enigma. She had a few friends back in the city but none that she considered close. They fell under the category more of classmates and acquaintances. She might miss one or two, and if she felt the need, she could always invite them out for a few days, but she also knew that they would not be happy outside of the city. They did not share her passions. In fact, she could have been much more popular if she was more interested in clothes or shopping.

Avery had three passions, animals, nature, and music. Her musical taste was not for the music that other people her age listened to though. At a very young age she fell in love with songs from The Beatles, The Eagles, Carole King, Dean Martin and even some of the early country singers. Influenced by her parents and grandparents, she had a very wide musical range. Avery tried to listen to the current music but found it so mundane and used that she always fell back on what she called real music. What they called classics. Infrequently, she would hear a song from a current singer or band that she liked and got so excited that she would find them on YouTube to listen to others they had recorded but was always disappointed. It would inevitably turn out to be, in her opinion, their one hit wonder. She was still hopeful that she would find another modern-day artist that could put together something with an actual melody but until then she would stick to the classics that she loved.

Avery finished arranging her room, stopped by her dad's office, and told him she was going exploring. He looked up at her and smiled. He knew she would enjoy it here and he was relieved to think that he had done the right thing by moving. Avery returned the smile and headed outside. She was immediately drawn to the trees and started singing as she walked among them. She had a beautiful singing voice and could carry a tune. A real tune, like a song from The Eagles or maybe Frank Sinatra. Avery knew it was silly, but she felt like the trees were listening to her and enjoying her company too. From her peripheral vision she thought she saw some kind of flying insect flit by her. It was too big for an insect, but it did not look like a bird. She swung around to see if she could catch what it was, but it was already gone. She started to walk in the direction of it but just then her dad called her for dinner.

The next morning Avery and her dad were up early. Her dad fixed breakfast for the two of them. Her stepmother, Marisa, was still sound asleep of course. She tended to sleep later these days. Marisa claimed it was because of the country air but Avery attributed it to the wine Marisa drank. Dave could tell his daughter was happy at the new house and Avery knew that while her dad loved the new place, he was still not completely happy with his marriage. Avery sincerely hoped that Marisa would turn out to be the wife that her dad wanted, and deserved, but unfortunately, she did not think that would happen. After breakfast, Avery went outside to visit the trees and her dad went to his office.

Avery made a beeline for the trees and began to serenade them again. That morning she started out with a Dean Martin classic, *Everybody Loves Somebody*. She walked over to the place where she thought she saw something rather large flit by her the previous day. There was nothing out of the ordinary there except the extreme beauty of the place. She knew that it was natural but some of the placement of the trees did not look accidental. It appeared that the denser areas surrounded a space that was almost park-like. They blocked out the surrounding neighbors. Inside the trees were still close but far enough apart to let sunshine in like moving, floating, spotlights, perfect for a performer on stage. Also, enough sunlight to support a plethora of wildflowers growing around the trees. These flowers were unattended by the previous owners, but they certainly look as if they were painstakingly planted because they were plentiful and beautiful.

Avery was floating around in the spotlights singing her

heart out when she noticed something in her peripheral vision again. This time she caught it in time but still could not identify it. She ran over to the tree where it disappeared and all she saw there was a very small hole too high up for her to peer into. Then just as she was trying to figure out what happened to her little mirage, she saw a squirrel run across a limb that she swore had something on its back. It was a bright color too. Must have been reflecting something from the sun. Maybe she was just imagining things, but she also felt like she was being watched. Somehow, she could tell it was not in a malicious way, just a curious way. It was not scary.

That night Avery went to bed, watched a little TV, read her book until she felt sleepy and then turned off her light for a good night's sleep. She was anxious to get back to the trees with a clear head.

Part 3

The next morning, after breakfast with her dad, she headed off to her trees. She selected a song and began to serenade them. As she was walking back to the house one of her stage spotlights, as she called them, fell beside a bush in the backyard. One of the rays caught a reflection of something shiny on the ground under the bush. What she found was very interesting. It looked like a part of a wing. A very delicate wing that, if it were whole, maybe over two inches wide. It was too big to be a dragonfly wing. She knew they could be pretty wide, but they were also narrower than these. Avery stared at it for the longest time and thought to herself that it could not be a real wing, it had to be off some kind of toy. The previous owners were elderly and had no grandkids so where would it have come from? Just then she noticed that there were several other wings and partial wings around the same area, some even caught in the bush. Avery was very careful as she collected them because they seemed so fragile. She collected five whole wings and several partial wings. Oddly enough, while she was collecting these, she could have sworn she saw several flitting movements out of her peripheral vision. She did not want to be distracted from what she was doing though because she had found several of these wings and if she looked away, she would lose sight of them. At this precise moment, the sun was shining just right for her to pick them out of the bushes and leaves. She stacked them all up gently, trying not to touch the inside of the fragile wings, cupped her hands together and carried them up to the house and into her room.

Avery put a couple of the wing fragments on a sheet of paper and carried them to her dad's office. The door was always open, but she knocked anyway. She showed her dad the wings and asked if he had ever seen anything like them. He looked them over carefully, never touching them though because he could also see that they looked fragile. Just like Avery, he admired the beauty and did not think they came from toys. They looked so real, but he could not imagine from whence they came. He was genuinely interested in them and that was just one of the many reasons that Avery loved her dad. They agreed that Avery had found something special and that she should keep investigating. So back to the trees she went.

As Avery walked among the trees, she was much more observant this time. She started noticing things she had not before, like the spacing of the trees themselves. Except for the narrow path, lined with bushes, leading into the park-like setting, the trees were very thick around the entire outer area. The inner area was also full of trees, but you could walk between them without a problem. In fact, Avery would 'do-si-do' among the trees while she was singing and dancing there. She noticed that within what she was calling the inner area, there were six very large trees that were spaced evenly around the circumference of this inner area. Avery wished that she knew more about trees and made a mental note to google them so she could identify them.

There was such a variety of trees, and she knew very little about them. She really only recognized a couple for sure, one was the weeping willows scattered around the area. The six huge trees that stood almost like sentinels she knew to be oak. They could possibly be hundreds of years old. They were majestic to say the least. Right beside each of the sentinel trees were what she found out later to be hawthorn trees. All were beautiful and all were magical in her opinion. All the while Avery was trying to study the trees, she again had the feeling she was also being observed like the trees themselves were studying her. A feeling like that should normally be disarming but for some reason it was oddly comforting for Avery. It was getting late so Avery gathered some leaves from the ground so she could identify some of the trees for tomorrow. She bid the area goodnight, walked up the path and into the house.

The next morning Avery went downstairs and was pleasantly surprised to see that Marisa was cooking breakfast. She said good morning to Marisa and her dad and Marisa declared it was time to eat. Avery sat down with her dad and Marisa served them both eggs, toast, and orange juice. They never ate a large breakfast. She enjoyed the small talk while they ate and even began to look at Marisa a little differently. Marisa was actually nice and genuinely happy. Marisa started loading the dishwasher as Dave went to his office and Avery went to her trees.

Avery walked among the trees lovingly touching each one. She was either talking or singing to them as she did. Again, that feeling of being watched, or maybe a better word would be studied, fell over her. She looked all around, stopping at every tree, just waiting for something, any kind of sign of something watching her. Then, in a normal voice, she said, "I know someone is here with me, watching me. I'm not afraid of you and you shouldn't be afraid of me either. Please let me see you so I know I'm not losing my mind." There was no response, but she did see, in her peripheral vision, several things moved quickly, all at once, all around. Still, she was not scared at all, maybe even a little relieved. Again, she pleaded, "Please, you have watched me, you know I mean you no harm. I want to meet you. I have to meet you. I know you are here."

Then she heard it. A very soft, very feminine, voice say, "Hello to you."

Avery whipped around at the sound and there on a branch just slightly above eye-level sat the most beautiful little being she had ever seen. She remembered how she fell in love with Tinkerbell the first time she saw her in that movie, but this little person was not a cartoon and was far more beautiful. She was tiny, maybe three inches tall, yet a perfect little person. Avery stood there staring with her mouth open until the little person snapped her tiny, dainty fingers to get Avery out of her trance.

"I'm so sorry to stare," Avery whispered.

"No problem," was the reply. "We need to talk, don't we?"

Avery could not believe what was happening, but she wanted this to be true. "My name is Avery," she said. "I have so many questions, but I know I will just start babbling so I'm going to let you start. Just know that I will never do anything to harm you or chase you away. I love that you are here."

"Thank you, Avery," she replied. "My name is Pippa."

Pippa's voice sounded to Avery like a beautiful song. She could detect a bit of what she thought might be an Irish lilt. It was elegant, graceful, dainty, delicate, and more adjectives that she could not think of at the moment. Avery understood how someone could be a little hypnotized by the sound alone. She could listen to her forever.

Pippa continued the conversation by answering some of the questions she knew that Avery had but was too dumbfounded at the time to ask. She told Avery that she was a fairy, and she was not alone. The Finagle was weakening fast but that was because of the previous landowners. She saw the look on Avery's face, so she automatically volunteered, "A Finagle is what a group of fairies is called, dear. Sometimes our groups are also called Frollicks or even just plain herds but personally I prefer Finagle." Pippa told her that the previous owners had booby-trapped the entire area and killed many fairies. She looked at Avery with tears in her gorgeous, tiny, eyes, and said, "We need help, and we need it fast. That's why we decided to put our faith in you. Please don't let us down."

Avery answered almost before Pippa had finished, "What do you need me to do?"

Part 4

Pippa confided to Avery that iron could be fatal for fairies and the previous owner had driven iron spikes in the ground and hung iron horseshoes in the trees around most of the fairy's doorways. She had driven iron spikes around the flowers and the tree trunks. This was all pure poison to the fairies. Worse yet, she had destroyed many of the fairy eggs. The fairies had been in this location for many, many, years but they would have to move and many of them were too weak to do that.

Avery told Pippa to show her where the iron was so she could get rid of it. Pippa flew to the nearest flowerbed and hovered above a spike barely visible within the flowers. Avery pulled it out of the ground, saw another one just inches away and pulled that out too. She pulled out twenty-eight spikes in just over an hour and piled them where she could take them away from the area completely. Then she had Pippa show her where the horseshoes were located.

Avery told Pippa she would need a couple things from the shed before she could get all the horseshoes, so she excused herself for a minute. She said, "Please don't go away Pippa, I will be right back. I just need to get a couple things from the shed."

A few minutes later Avery returned with a claw

hammer, a ladder, and a couple of empty burlap sacks. She went to the pile of iron spikes and put them in one of the burlap sacks then she ran back over to Pippa for directions to all the horseshoes. Pippa showed her where they were hidden on the ground first and Avery gathered them. After finding a few Avery started to notice them, along with more spikes, and it seemed as if there were dozens of them, everywhere. For the horseshoes that were in the trees Avery needed the ladder and the claw hammer. They were nailed to the trees, and she noticed that the horseshoes were all nailed around small holes. She gathered all the horseshoes and spikes and put them all in the burlap sacks. Avery swore to Pippa that she would get every one of them out. It was getting late, and Avery's dad had just called her to supper so she told Pippa she would be back in the morning. Pippa thanked her and told her to get some rest that they had a lot of talking to do.

Avery dragged the heavy burlap bags into the shed. She was exhausted, sweaty, and dirty when she went into the house for supper. Her dad looked at her and told her she must have been working hard out among the trees and Avery told him it was a wonderful day. She ate more than she had in a long time, went upstairs, took a shower, and went to bed. She was asleep almost immediately, but she was happy. So happy.

Part 5

The next morning Avery bounded from her bed, got dressed, and raced downstairs. She was going to bypass breakfast, but her dad stopped her in the hallway and insisted she eat with him. He could tell she was anxious to get outside. They sat at the table, looked at each other and smiled. Avery knew that her dad was more satisfied there than he was in the city and his marriage looked promising as well. Dave knew that this was the happiest he had seen Avery since her mom died. That made him happy.

Avery raced out to the trees. She could not wait to see Pippa. She went to the spot where they had first met, and she was not there. Avery quietly called for her. She walked over to the nearest Hawthorn tree just in time to see Pippa emerge from a very small hole a little above her eye level, in the tree. She remembered she had removed a horseshoe from that very spot just the previous day. Pippa flew onto the nearest limb and thanked Avery again saying, "Because of you, Avery, we can now use all our portals. We all give you dearest thanks. You have earned our trust so a couple others can't wait to meet you." Right then, two more fairies emerged from the hole. "Avery, I would like to introduce you to Fawn and Elga."

Avery was so excited she could not contain herself. These little people were so delicate and beautiful. "It is my pleasure to meet you," she said.

Fawn flew right up to Avery and landed on her shoulder, but Elga was missing a large part of one wing and unable to fly. Avery noticed this right away and said, "Oh Elga, I'm so sorry, what happened to your beautiful wing?" Before she could answer Avery had extended her arm as a bridge for Elga to join Fawn on her shoulder. Elga jumped on her arm and ran up to her shoulder as Avery sat down on the grass in preparation for a long talk.

Elga started to respond but then she bowed her head and let out a little sigh. She started to cry.

Pippa jumped up to respond instead with, "Avery, the woman who lived here before you was very mean to us. You already know about all the iron but that was not all she did to our little community. We were so sorry that she discovered us. She made a hobby out of torturing us. Clearly, she was trying to get rid of us. She hated us. I don't know why. She would try to catch us and if she did, I think she killed us. We watched her crush one friend with an iron spike and it wasn't long after, that a few of our extended family members went missing. Other times she would just be able to catch one of us by our wings and yank real hard.

That's what happened to Elga. Fortunately, Elga was flung far enough away when she yanked on her wing that she couldn't find her. If she had, she would have killed her."

Fawn's little voice then piped in with "We have several injured like Elga. Avery, why would someone do that to us?"

Avery was in tears. This was so sad. She went from thinking the people who lived in the house before them were good people, to hating them, at least the woman, and glad she was dead. Through her sobs she choked out, "Oh Gah, I'm so, so, sorry." It was hard to understand but they knew what she meant.

The three fairies gathered around Avery. Elga was on one shoulder, Fawn was on the other and Pippa hopped onto her lap and the three of them found themselves patting Avery and consoling her. This made Avery cry even harder since she was the one that should be consoling them. They were the ones that were attacked by that wicked woman.

Avery was a mess. She reached in her pocket for an ever-present paper towel, wiped her eyes, blew her nose, then looked at the beautiful, delicate fairies consoling her and said, "I collected some wings and wing parts from the yard the other day, and I know this might be a stupid question but is there some way you could reattach them? Don't you have a little magic that you could use to do that?"

Pippa flew up, hovered about five inches from Avery's face and said, "You found our wings? You really found our wings?"

"Yes," said Avery, "The other day the sun was shining on them just right, and for maybe just a second or two, if that hadn't happened, I would have never seen them. It was pure luck that I saw them in the first place because within seconds the sun wasn't shining on them the same and all signs of them were gone. The ones that I carefully collected are in my room, safe and sound."

Part 6

It was obvious that Pippa was excited that some wings and/or wing parts had been found, and by someone as trustworthy as Avery. She decided it was time for her to answer all of Avery's Fairy questions by giving her a brief lesson. She told Avery that she would get to the wing question after she had finished telling her a little about Fairies. Elga and Fawn were still on Avery's shoulders so they both sat down while Pippa hopped on one of Avery's crossed legs and sat down.

Pippa began by telling Avery that their little family, or colony, included both fairies, elves, and elflings, offspring of elves and fairies. Since Avery had only met three of them, all fairies, Pippa wanted to prepare her for meeting the rest of the family. She told her that fairies can represent distinctive parts of nature. This family was more like garden fairies. All fairies can fly, and some can even fly without wings. In their case this was not true though so when their wings are damaged, or mauled, through attacks of some kind, it hinders them from flying. She told her that fairies have powers and can be an immense help to humans with anything from healing them to warning them of impending danger. On the other hand, they can also use their powers to harm humans, but this was a power that was never taken lightly, and very rarely used.

Pippa could see that Avery was taking in all this information with intense interest. She continued her little talk to include the elflings in the family. She told Avery that elves are amazing. They do not have wings, but elves can talk to plants and animals. Sometimes they would hitch a ride on a squirrel or a bird. The elves had many powers. They were healers, sages, witches, and wizards, and because they could talk to plants, they were incredible alchemists. Elves are also remarkable craftsmen and can create things with their hands that humans could never attempt. Elves trust humans even less than fairies do so they rarely mingle with them, but the elves in this family agreed to meet with Avery at some point.

Pippa took a breath and said, "Avery, we are putting our lives in danger by trusting you, but we all agreed, and I do believe we have chosen wisely. If humans ever know of us, it is most likely because we have allowed this to happen, but it was not what happened with that horrid woman. We can be very involved in human lives if we choose and our experience with humans will stay with us forever and be a determining factor on whether we choose to interact with them ever again. It should have been a very tough choice to ever trust humans again after the previous occupants, but you made it easy."

"Remember I mentioned that our elves are remarkable craftsmen and can create and fix things?" Avery nodded. Pippa continued with, "I want to see if our elves can possibly fix and reattach the wing and wing parts that you collected. I'm so glad that you found them because we saw that horrid woman crush some and took the rest, we assumed to destroy."

Avery was still weepy when she said, "Pippa, Fawn, Elga, I can't apologize enough for what a human has done to you. That witch must have dropped these in the backyard and then couldn't find them. It embarrasses me to think someone is capable of that. I can't believe that you would trust me after that. I couldn't blame you if you didn't, I don't think I would have if I were one of you, but I'm so glad you chose to trust me."

Pippa continued, "We have been here for many, many, years without incident. We were here years before the previous owners, and they were here for years before they discovered us but when they did things quickly went south. It was the woman that discovered us. I don't know why she even came back here in the first place. She usually tended to the flowers in the front of the house or the vegetable garden directly behind the house. We had gotten lax back here, more than comfortable being out and about, when that woman came through the bushes and saw many of us working in the flowers and buzzing about. She screamed at us and started grabbing at us and swatting everywhere. She connected with several fairies and either crushed or pulled their wings off. Worst of all, she killed one of us, while we watched." Pippa started sobbing and her voice was cracking as she added, "She stomped on Fern." After that statement, Elga, Fawn and Pippa were all quietly sobbing. Avery was also crying.

"The next day the woman came back with a bag full of iron horseshoes and spikes," said Pippa. "I think she went home that first night and did all kinds of research on how to hurt or kill us. Fortunately, most of our eggs were under leaves that were out of her reach, even with a ladder, or she would have destroyed all of them too. I can't understand why she hated us so much. We did nothing to her; all we did was make this land back here beautiful. She never had to plant a flower back here, we did it all. She never came back here, and I guess she thought all these beautiful flowers and flowerbeds were wild."

"I'm going to run up to the house and get your wings right now," said Avery. Then she added, "Would any of you like to come to the house with me?"

"Would it be safe?" Pippa asked.

"Well, you and Fawn could fly up to the second story window on the right, that's my room, and I could carry Elga in the hood of my sweatshirt. My dad is in his office and my stepmother is probably reading or in the kitchen," said Avery. "They should both be downstairs, I would go directly upstairs but I would protect you from anything, I want you to believe that. I thought you might be curious."

Elga chimed in with, "Oh, Avery, we do trust you, believe me, and I have been dying to go inside a real people house. I'll be very quiet; you won't even know I'm here. Please take us."

Pippa volunteered then with, "Yes, we have always been curious." Then she choked up a little as she added, "One day

Fern and I flew up to the window just to look inside but we didn't stay long, too scared, and we know now it was rightfully so."

"I still can't understand how anyone could have that much hate," said Avery. "I will keep you safe. Elga will go with me, and I will open the window for you and Fawn."

Part 7

Avery got up and opened her hood for Elga to step inside then she started toward the house. Inside the house she was heading toward the stairs when her dad called out to her from his office. She walked into his office to find both he and Marisa. This was unusual. They both appeared to be in a good mood. Her dad asked if she would like to run into town with them. Evidently, they were going to go visit some of the antique shops in town and asked if she would like to come along. Avery gracefully declined and added that she was planting some new flowers in the back and wanted to get that done today. She was glad to see that they seemed happy though and were doing something together for a change. She knew that made her dad happy.

Avery walked them to the garage. Marisa said, "We are going to bring something home for supper, what would you like?"

Avery answered with, "Surprise me. I'm sure whatever you decide will be good for me. Have fun."

Avery waved to them as they pulled out of the driveway then ran upstairs to her room. She opened the window and called out, "Hey guys sorry it took so long, It's all clear now."

Pippa and Fawn flew in the window then and sat on the dresser where Avery had placed Elga. "Please make yourselves comfortable," said Avery. "Look around and help yourself to anything you like. Elga, I will carry you anywhere you want to go."

Avery walked over to her desk, opened a drawer, and pulled out a stack of papers. She carefully peeled a few pages off the stack and the wings were still displayed on the next page. They were still placed just as she had placed them so no further harm would come to them. Pippa flew over and exclaimed, "Oh, Avery, they look wonderful! You can tell that you have taken great care in preserving them!"

"I was very careful," answered Avery. "I just knew they were something magical and not simple trash. Even if I had not met you, I would have kept these safe forever."

Pippa landed on the desk near the wings and examined them closely for what seemed like a long time before she looked up at Elga and said, "Elga, I think this is your wing, and I believe the elves will be able to mend you."

Avery placed Elga on the desk near the wings and Elga started crying. She exclaimed, "Oh, Pippa, it is! It's mine! And I recognize the others as well! I know we will be whole again!"

Pippa looked up at Avery and said, "Avery, I cannot, no, we cannot thank you enough for this. After looking closely at these wings, I am certain that you have given the gift of flight back to at least five fairies and possibly six. We have two fairies that have lost both their wings and Elga who had lost one. We also have two fairies who have lost partial wings and I believe that these four partials that you have collected will be the missing parts that they need to be whole. Our entire family will be eternally grateful to you for what you have done for us."

"I think there may have been even more wing fragments, maybe I should search for more," said Avery.

Pippa answered with, "There is no need, Avery. If there are more, they belonged to fairies that were killed."

Part 8

Marisa and Dave walked hand in hand as they entered one of the little antique stores in town. Behind the counter stood a man checking out another customer. He wore a bold, beautiful, royal blue, polo shirt that accented his brilliant blue eyes, and a pair of jeans. His looks were casual, masculine, and distinguished. He smiled and nodded at the couple and told them to feel free to look around but if they needed help to just yell. He also pointed to a table against the wall with fresh coffee and cookies. The shop was small but very busy. Busy in two ways, both with people and with merchandise. They were both still finding amazing things to look at when the man behind the counter came around and said, "Hi. I apologize for not coming over sooner but my helper is out today so it's just me here. My name is Mark. Is there anything I can help you with?" Up close it was clear to see that Mark was a little older than he looked from a distance. The way he stood and moved from afar he could pass for someone in their twenties, but up close they could see that he was around their age, mid-thirties. Very distinguished but still down to earth and normal.

"Hi," responded Dave. "I'm Dave and this is Marisa. Nice to meet you."

Marisa added, "We love your shop. I could stay here all day."

"Thank you, Marisa," said Mark, "that is exactly the remark I love to hear! Are you looking for anything in particular?"

Dave took over then and said, "I agree with my wife, you have some beautiful objects here but today I am kind of looking for something for my daughter. She is such a good kid, never asks for anything, always happy, fascinated with nature and sometimes the supernatural."

"Oh, well, I'm sure we can find something here," said Mark, "I have been all around the world and only buy authentic treasures from exciting places. When you say supernatural, I have items ranging from religions, like voodoo, to what some just consider magical."

"Oh no," answered Dave, "she's more of a lighthearted soul. She's infatuated with the pegasus, or little elves, or basically anything with wings. She also loves trees and flowers and all of nature. So I guess we should look at what you call magical."

"I think I have just the thing!" said Mark. "I got in a shipment that included these extraordinary music boxes. I started putting them out just today, but I remember one that had the most beautiful fairy on it. Do you think she would be interested in that?"

"I believe you hit the nail on the head, Mark!" replied Dave. "She has a little fairy collection. Like I said, anything with wings, real or magic, whether it exists, or doesn't!"

Mark went in the back and returned carrying a small box. He said, "This is an antique music box with a fairy instead of the obligatory ballerina on it. I thought it was very unique." He opened the box and inside was a tiny porcelain fairy with diaphanous wings. She was less than two inches tall and sat on a small wooden frame. Mark carefully wound the tiny protruding button on the back and the fairy started slowly spinning and moving up and down to the music of a nocturne by Chopin.

"What do you think?" asked Mark.

"Avery will love it," answered Dave, "we'll take it."

"I have a proposition for you," said Mark.

Dave looked at him and said, "I'm listening?"

"Let me give this to Avery as a gift," began Mark, "in exchange for dinner. My treat of course."

"I agree to the gift for Avery," answered Dave, "but the dinner, absolutely not. You will come to our house for dinner."

"I am new here," added Mark, "and I've been busy with the shop. I've not met anyone here yet and am starving for some adult conversation."

Marisa added, "And a home cooked meal too, I hope! We are also new to the area, just moved here a couple months ago."

Mark stuck out his hand and gave Dave a firm, new friend, handshake and said, "It's a deal!" He then offered his hand to Marisa and she reciprocated in the same fashion. It was the beginning of a friendship. "Do you live here in the village?"

"No, but not far, about three miles out," said Dave.

Mark looked at him and asked, "Did you happen to buy that land where the elderly couple had lived? I believe the woman died."

"Yes, how did you know that?" asked Dave.

"Because I also looked at that area before I moved into the village," said Mark. "But since I had my shop I bought this place with the apartment upstairs, much easier for me, but I remember that house with the gorgeous yard."

Later that day, Avery almost cried when Dave and Marisa gave her the music box. "It's so beautiful," she cried. "She's so tiny. I love it you guys! Thank you so much!"

"You have to thank Mark for that," said Dave, "It's really a gift from him and you can thank him tomorrow night, he's coming to dinner."

"I will," she said, "I will."

Late that afternoon Avery took her new music box out to her garden. Pippa gave a little excited scream when she saw it and said, "Oh Avery, look at her! So pretty! And look, when I stand by her, I feel like a giant! Play the music again, it's pretty too, but honestly Avery, I think we have all loved hearing you sing. I don't think we have heard a bad song from you yet!" Soon there were several fairies standing by the tiny porcelain figure. They were giggling and standing by it so they all felt like giants. They loved it. Avery made a mental note that she would have to get some kind of similar music box just for them, so they could play with it whenever they wanted.

Over the next two weeks Mark and Dave became fast friends, visiting each other almost daily. Dave and Marisa loved so many things in Mark's shop and they felt guilty when he wanted to give them deals on everything. Mark was over for dinner several times a week. They thoroughly enjoyed each other's company. Avery noticed the change in her dad, and in Marisa. Avery was friendly with Mark, of course, but it took her a while to trust him. She loved her new music box and put it in a place of honor in her room. Right between two beautiful figurines, one of another fairy, and one of a winged horse.

Even though Mark was much older than her, he was her dad's age, Avery could still recognize his good looks. Avery had just begun to accept Marisa and prayed that she was not interested in him in that way but after a few weeks of seeing them all together, her fears were happily quelled. She found it hard to believe but she had to admit that she liked Marisa now. They talked, laughed, shared feelings, she realized that Marisa loved her dad, and she was happy to have someone to talk to about certain things again. Though she tried not to, and she remained apprehensive, she had become friends with Marisa.

Part 9

Avery was out with the fairies every day. The fairies never hid when they saw Avery coming, instead, they went to greet her. They taught her how to plant flowers and talk to all the animals and the trees. Avery commented on the flowers, "These are the most beautiful flowers I think I've ever seen. They look like jester hats or maybe upside-down trumpets, or I don't know what, I just can't even describe them."

Pippa laughed and said, "These are columbine plants and yes, they are definitely different. Sometimes you look at them and think lilies or even pansies or maybe think they're like a combination of several different flowers. Hard to describe, aren't they?"

"That's just what I was thinking!" said Avery. "I don't know how I would describe these to anyone. I don't remember ever seeing these before, are they common around here?"

"Columbine plants are common in this area but some of what you are seeing is not," said Pippa. She pointed to a couple of flowers. One was multicolored and the other was brilliant royal blue with other various shades of blue in it. "Now, these two flowers are not indigenous to this area. These are some of our fairy flowers. You won't see these in anyone's yard, any flower shop, or out with other wildflowers. These are fairy favorites that you will only see where fairies do their gardening, we made these again just for you."

"They are fantastic, Pippa. Thank you for putting these out here," said Avery.

"Thank you for helping us, Avery," replied Pippa, "You are truly a very good friend."

Avery was learning so much from the fairies. Because the animals were friends of fairies, Avery was even able to interact sometimes with squirrels, rabbits, and even a family of foxes. Since the fairies were always out now with no fear of Avery, she decided they better have a warning signal of some kind for when someone else came out into this area. The fairies already had elves stationed by the bushes at the entrance to the back area. They alerted everyone when someone, or something, strange was entering the area. Avery knew that her dad wanted to visit the area that she practically called home now so she told Pippa she would whistle or something to alert the elves at the entrance so they could pass it along.

It was a good thing they had discussed this because the very next day Avery's dad and Marisa told her they were going to go with her to see her little paradise. Avery ran ahead and as she approached the bushes she whistled and yelled "HERE WE ARE!" Dave and Marisa just thought she was excited at them seeing this part of her world but if they had been closer, they would have been able to see all the bustling and hiding going on there. Avery showed her dad and Marisa the flowers that she had worked on, the areas where she sang, and she named almost all the trees in the inner area. They were impressed by the beauty. Avery told them things about the trees, butterflies, squirrels, rabbits, plants, and flowers. It seemed like she had something to teach them about everything in her area. Dave was amazed that Avery had learned so much, about so much, in only a couple months but he guessed it was because she was so happy there. It was also obvious that the small animals only shied away because of Dave and Marisa, not Avery.

"We've got to bring Mark out here, if that okay Avery," asked Dave. "He would love it too. All these flowers, when did you ever find the time to plant them?"

"Dad, these are mostly wildflowers that were already here," answered Avery. "I may have transplanted some or moved some. I wish I could take credit for this, but it is nature at its finest."

"Yes, it is," said Marisa. "It's gorgeous, Avery. I'm so proud of you. The beauty of this place almost brings tears to my eyes. I can see why this is the inspiration for some of the beautiful and original braids that you fix in your hair. And I don't see a mirror."

Avery looked at Marisa and said, "Oh, but I do have a mirror out here. And I have my little portable karaoke machine and some other stuff out here in that little box there by the big tree in the middle. I like to sing out here and I can really cut loose!" But she had to stifle a laugh because the braids that Marisa spoke of were the labors of the fairies. Three or four of them would grab some of her long hair and weave. They would fly up and around and through to create some of the most intricate weaves. Avery wished she could have a video. It must have been quite a comical, and magical, sight.

Avery walked them back to the house and as she went through the opening in the bushes into the backyard, without even thinking, she called out, "I'll be back later!"

Dave and Marisa looked at each other and laughed. Dave looked at Avery and said, "Do you think they're going to leave or something?" Avery laughed along.

The next day Mark came for dinner, but he did not come alone. He was quite a regular there for dinner so when he came, he just walked in the door and announced, "It's me, and I have a surprise."

This got Dave and Marisa's attention so they both went to the living room to see Mark standing there with a very attractive woman holding a beautiful bouquet of flowers. He said, "I hope you don't mind that I brought company. This is Nikki. She manages the new shop in the village. I asked her out to dinner but I forgot I was having dinner here so I didn't think you would mind if I brought her."

"Of course not," said Marisa, "It's good to meet you Nikki, please come on in and make yourself at home. Mark is already at home here so I'll show you to the kitchen where we can have a drink before dinner."

"These are for you," said Nikki as she handed the bouquet to Marisa. The bouquet consisted of about eleven white, or cream colored, beautiful flowers but there was one flower that stood out from the rest, it was an exquisite blue with several different shades of blue within it. Marisa poured them each a glass of wine and they started a conversation of small talk as she put the flowers in a vase and placed them in the middle of the counter. Marisa put the pasta in a pot of boiling water then went over to the back door and called Avery for dinner.

A few minutes later Avery ran into the house and up the stairs and announced, "I'm gonna go wash up, be down in a few!" Avery ran up the stairs and into her room. Most days she left the window open so the fairies could fly in and out and explore everywhere in her room. Her dad or Marisa rarely had any reason to come upstairs. If they happened to come up unexpectedly while the fairies were inside there were plenty of places for them to hide. Avery had pulled books out far enough so they could hide comfortably behind them in the bookcase and since Avery had so many little fairy pictures and statuettes, they may even be able to hide right out in the open. There was never a problem though because Dave or Marisa never snooped. Avery loved that about them.

Part 10

When Avery entered her room Pippa and Fawn were waiting for her. She said, "They're here and I'm betting they'll want to come out to what they call my secret garden so did you get everyone hidden?"

"Don't worry Avery," said Fawn.

Pippa joined in with, "Yeah, you worry about us too much! Everything is hidden. It's still a beautiful garden but with less wildlife." She giggled a little at that.

Avery snickered at that too and said, "You guys are welcome to stay here. You can listen to the radio or turn on the TV, as long as you don't play it too loud."

Pippa said, "We know you let us have the run of things here but I think it might be best if we're out in your secret garden, making sure some things stay secret. I'm sure we'll see you later. Avery, have fun though, don't worry!"

In the kitchen as Avery went by in a blur, Marisa smiled at Nikki and said, "That's my stepdaughter Avery. She isn't happy unless she is out with the trees, flowers, and animals. Our girl is definitely outdoorsy! She'd much rather be outside than in."

"That's just like I was when I was a young girl," said Nikki.

Marisa laughed and said, "Not me! I was city through and through but now I wish I had been raised in a place like this. I have to admit though, since Dave and I moved here I have begun to appreciate the outdoors more. I really never took a minute to look at the beauty, and I have Dave and Avery to thank for making me see it. I never would have thought it but I'm so glad that we moved here now."

"You have a beautiful home," said Nikki. "I'm city girl all the way but I could maybe get used to a home like yours."

The men walked into the kitchen area, set their glasses on the table, and Dave said, "The menfolk are ready for dinner."

Marisa and Nikki both looked at them and laughed.

Dave looked at Mark and said, "See Mark, I told you I don't get any respect here."

He looked around and said, "Is Avery in yet?"

"Yes, she's washing up, she'll be down any time now," said Marisa.

As if on cue, Avery walked into the kitchen and Dave said, "Avery, we have a guest tonight, meet Nikki."

Avery nodded at Nikki and said, "Nice to meet you Nikki." Nikki reciprocated.

They all gathered around the counter for the buffet style meal. Marisa placed the dishes on the counter and said, "Okay, everyone grab a plate." Then she looked at Mark and said, "So, Mark, how did you and Nikki meet?"

Mark answered, "Well, Nikki just moved here and she's working at that new dress shop in town."

"Listen to him, Marisa," said Nikki, "Just like a man. It's a fashion boutique. It's a specialty store or maybe you could call it a shoppe with that extra pe on the end of shop," she laughed as she said that "The name says it all, it's Haute Couture."

"Excuse me," laughed Mark, "I'm just a hick with a store that has old shit for sale. I don't know about this high fashion stuff."

Even Avery laughed at that. She had become friends with Mark and enjoyed his company. They had bonded over karaoke and chess. She had her karaoke out a while back and Mark joined her in harmony to one of her Beatles songs. She got so excited that they sang together for the next three hours straight. Dave and Marisa told them they were great, and they felt like they were attending a concert. Avery was surprised that Mark liked all the same songs. Then they discovered that they both like chess, as well. Avery added, "Oh Mark, we'll always have our karaoke, and I might even let you beat me at chess!"

Marisa relocated the vase to make room on the counter for the dishes. She said, "Avery, did you see the beautiful flowers that Nikki brought?"

"They're very pretty," said Avery.

They all started filling their plates and Dave added, "I think those are like some of those out in your little world, aren't they?"

"They're columbine plants," answered Avery. She glanced over and noticed a slight change in Nikki. It was like she was holding her breath, just waiting for more information from Avery. It was odd but Avery was suspicious of anything that might expose her friends. The flowers that Nikki had brought were all common except the blue one. This one was not common. It had been created by fairies. "Those in my world, as you call it, are like most of these but the blue one, it's different. I've not seen this kind before."

"Are you sure, Avery?" asked Marisa. "I remember some that seemed so different, the colori..."

Before she could finish her sentence Avery cut her off and said, "Nope, that one's definitely different, trust me." She noticed that Nikki was very intently watching Avery's reaction to the flowers. She glanced at Nikki and swore she had a reaction that could only be described as fear. It was the way her eyebrows flinched every so brief but enough that Avery saw something. She knew there was something very wrong here, something not right with Nikki. Why was she here? Avery did not think it was because of Mark. He was just the way to get here. She had to talk to Pippa. While everyone was eating and talking, she got up to get a drink and secretly took a picture of the flowers with her phone.

Avery took her plate to the sink and announced, "I left my karaoke outside, I'm gonna go get it real quick. I forgot to put it in my little box out there and Mark might just want to show off his singing skills tonight, anyway, I'll be right back."

As soon as Avery hit the back porch she started running. As she went through the bushes she whispered for the elves to be on the lookout in case someone was following her. When she reached the big tree in the middle she quietly called out for Pippa. It took no time at all for Pippa to appear. Avery told her about Nikki and her bouquet and showed her the picture.

"She can't have that flower! That blue one was made by fairies!" cried Pippa. "By us! Here! How can she have that? Oh, this is bad Avery."

"That's why I'm telling you. I was suspicious from the very start, it was like she expected me to identify those flowers and I didn't," said Avery. "Maybe you should hide the flowers that you created for a while, just in case she gets out here. Don't worry, I would never invite her but I'm thinking she already knew what was here. I got to get back to the house but I had to warn you." She grabbed her karaoke machine and ran back to the house.

"Thank you Avery," called Pippa. Avery waved in response.

Avery ran inside with the karaoke machine and Dave said, "I don't think Mark's gonna want to karaoke tonight, Avery."

"That's okay," said Avery, "I needed to bring it in anyway, I don't want it to get rained on and I think it's starting to sprinkle."

Mark looked over at Avery and said, "Avery, I hope you don't mind but I told Nikki about the fairy music box you have. Evidently, you and Nikki share the same interests. She loves fairies too. Do you think she could see it?"

Avery smiled and said, "Of course, Mark. I'll go get it."

She carried her prize carefully down the stairs, walked over to Nikki and said, "The only way this could be better is if it was real, or if it was riding on a winged horse, a pegasus."

Avery knew that she would never betray the trust of Pippa and her group so she had to play the little girl role here and seem more excited about them. In reality, she was over the moon excited about them, and she had every reason to be, but in this scenario, she had to play an excited young girl about make-believe stuff.

Avery set the music box on the counter and wound the stem. The little lights went on and the tiny fairy started turning to the music of Chopin. Nikki looked at it and said, "Oh Avery, this is beautiful. Absolutely gorgeous! She's so tiny."

"I always guessed that would be about their real size, this tiny and petite," Avery laughed. "Can you imagine a few of these fussing around your garden? Wouldn't that be great? She looks so fragile. Wouldn't that be neat if she could just come alive? I could take her back to my garden. I think she would love it there with all the flowers and rabbits and squirrels. Then if this came true, I would like a few winged horses, as well."

"So, you don't believe these actually exist, right?" asked Nikki.

Avery jerked her head around to look directly in Nikki's eyes. Avery's eyes had widened to the size of half dollars as she looked at Nikki. After just a second her eyes narrowed and she laughed a little as she said, "I know you'll think I'm foolish but I have, on more than one occasion, pretended these, and other, little beings existed. Daydreamed about them. Mark says you love them too, so you can't really tell me that you've never wished they would be real, can you?"

"I've gone so far as to hallucinate them right in front of me," said Nikki.

"Isn't that kind of the same as daydream?" asked Avery.

"I think it seems a little more real," answered Nikki. "I found something you should see, Avery. Mark and I have been invited to a barbecue with you and your family this Saturday. I will bring something special for you to see."

Avery had done exactly what she wanted to do. She may have earned the trust of Nikki and she was terrified.

Part 11

The next day Avery woke up earlier than usual and made her way to her garden in the back. After gathering Pippa and at least twenty other fairies and elves around her, she began to tell them about Nikki. She assured them she had given an academy award deserving performance to get Nikki's trust, but she did not know what to do next.

Avery's eyes were wet as she said, "They're coming out Saturday and they're gonna want to see my world, your world, so you need to hide everything for a while. I'm so sorry but I won't be able to stop them. Watch that woman, that Nikki, she is not to be trusted, and yet, there's something about her I believe. She actually seems to trust me and for some crazy reason, I trust a part of her. It's like she's scared of something else, not fairies. I honestly believe that she is telling me the truth but there's something hidden there and it scares the shit out of me. It ain't right. Try to hide anything and everything that would give her any clue that fairies exist here. I know you can use something called glamours to make people think they see what they don't and vice versa. Maybe you can do something to her to prove there is nothing out here except beautiful plants and animals. Please, please, hide everything. Hide your doorways, your flowers, yourselves. I'm sorry. I'm so sorry. This woman knew about this place before she came here. I just know she did. Maybe she's just using Mark. I believe he is innocent. Hopefully he's not in love. Aw shit! I don't like this at all. I hope you don't leave for good but I wouldn't blame you."

Pippa jumped in and said, "Don't worry Avery, there will be no signs of us at all. You are such a good friend and we have felt so safe here. I don't think we need to pack up just yet. You know, we aren't entirely defenseless so please don't worry about us, at least not just yet."

On Saturday, the day of the barbecue, Avery was a mess. She was a mix of emotions. She was mad, anxious, and terrified. She was afraid she was putting her new friends in danger. She was very quiet, and very near tears, when she went to visit Pippa and the others. She sat down by the large middle tree. Even with her head down, Avery could tell that she was being surrounded. Fairies landed on and around her. Elves were soon gathered as well, some on the backs of squirrels or rabbits. It could have been a picture right out of a fairy-tale storybook if it had not been so solemn.

"Avery," said Elga, "You don't have the weight of the world on your shoulders. Please share. Look at all of us! We're here for you! We're here because of you!" There were agreement murmurings among the others. "Avery, without you, I would not be able to fly again. Without you, we would not be able to live here anymore because you removed all the iron."

Fawn agreed and said, "She's right Avery. We won't let you feel guilty about this."

"Look at everyone here to support you, Avery!" added Pippa. "Everyone here knows that you are a great protector. Did I ever tell you what your name, Avery, means? It means wise, ruler of elves and fairies. What a happy coincidence, or is it? I think we knew you were our best friend when we first met. Now we just need to convince you. Like I told you before, we are not defenseless, in fact, we are quite an army to contend with now that the iron is gone. Just as you protect us, we will always protect you. We are in this together and remember, this is not necessarily even a problem. It is always better to be safe than sorry, though."

"In other words," said Fawn, "don't worry. We got this. We don't sweat the small shit."

This elicited laughs all around. A very good way to end a meeting.

Dave was busy getting all the barbecue paraphernalia out and ready for dinner while Marisa was busy in the kitchen preparing side dishes. Avery wandered in and asked her if she needed any help. Marisa smiled a very big smile and said, "I've been looking forward to this so I think I have everything that can be fixed early already done but I really appreciate you asking." Avery could see the drastic change in Marisa from when they were living in the city. Marisa was actually happy.

"If you change your mind, let me know," said Avery, but she still hung around the kitchen.

Marisa could tell it looked like something was on her mind, so she asked, "Avery, do you need to talk about something? Or maybe not need to, but maybe just want to talk about something? I can tell there's something on your mind. You know you can unload on me."

Avery looked at her and smiled. She loved that Marisa was interested in her. It had been a long time since she had an older woman to talk to about anything. She still missed her mom. It had been five years since she was able to talk to a mother-like figure and she had a lot more going on now than she did when she was six years old. She wanted to tell Marisa that she appreciated her, but she was still not totally open to talk to her like her real Mom. She said, "I haven't told you lately but I've seen a big change in you, and in Dad. You both seem happy, and that makes me happy."

"Avery," answered Marisa, "I am happy. I didn't think I would like it out here but I was wrong, very wrong. I love it. I was a city girl my whole life but that's because I never knew anything else. I didn't know I would love it out here. I love your dad. I don't want to scare you off but I believe I'm falling in love with you too. You are amazing. I admire you so much. I think, no, I know I feared you at first because of the closeness between you and your dad. I admired that but it scared me because I felt like I may never be included. I'm still an outsider, I know that, but it feels like it's getting better. Am I right?"

Avery could see that this was tough on Marisa. She could tell that she choked up a little and there were tears just about ready to fall from her eyes. She walked over to Marisa, hugged her, and answered, "Yes." Marisa hugged her back, they both had tears, and Avery could feel her heart grow.

Part 12

Mark and Nikki arrived around 1:00 pm for the barbecue. Mark walked in and announced their arrival. Mark and Nikki were holding hands as they entered the kitchen and said hello to Marisa and Avery. Mark was carrying beer and Nikki had a decorative paper bag that she put down in the living room. Mark said, "I better go help Dave with the cooler," as he laughed and made his escape.

Nikki asked, "What can I do to help?" Avery noticed that she did not sound like herself, there was something just a little off about her.

"No, no, you are a guest," said Marisa, "Avery and I have it all ready."

"That's not true," added Avery, "Marisa did it all."

"Believe me, Avery," said Marisa, "you have been a huge help this morning." They smiled at each other then looked over at Nikki. "Are you okay? You seem a little quiet today."

"I'm fine," answered Nikki, "guess I didn't sleep well or something. Just a little off today, but once I get going I'll be fine. Thanks for asking though. It's been a while since I've had any close friends. I mean friends that know me well enough to even know if I am a little off, let alone ask me about it. It's nice."

"Nikki," volunteered Avery, "You know you're welcome here and of course we are all friends. Besides, you're my fairy sister. We love the same things, that proves we are friends." Avery felt funny as she said that because while she was still suspicious of Nikki, for some reason she wanted to be her friend. She had mixed feelings about her but above all, her loyalties were with the fairies.

Nikki walked over to Marisa and Avery, wiped her eyes a little, then said, "I can't tell you how much it means that you would call me your friend. It's been a long time since I've had any kind of relationship, I mean good relationship, and it feels good."

That is when Avery noticed a dark spot on Nikki's left

cheek. It was somewhat covered with makeup but some must had been wiped off when Nikki wiped her eyes. Avery said, "What is that Nikki? Do you have a bruise on your cheek? Where, how did you get that? What happened?"

Nikki quickly covered her cheek and said, "Oh, it's nothing. I think I hit it accidentally. I'm fine. It's okay."

"I don't think it's okay," added Marisa, "what happened to you? Please tell me it wasn't Mark."

Nikki interrupted before Marisa even finished with, "No, no, no, please don't even think that! Mark is the best thing that has ever happened to me! Just know that it wasn't Mark and it was a total accident. He hasn't even seen it. I'm clumsy. Please don't mention it to Mark. I need to go freshen up a little." Nikki appeared as if she might spill more tears so she excused herself quickly to go to the bathroom.

Marisa and Avery looked at each other. "What the hell?" Marisa asked.

"There's certainly more there than she is telling, isn't there?" asked Avery.

"Yes, poor thing," answered Marisa. "So, what do we do? She made it clear that Mark didn't do it or that he doesn't even know about it. Should we just keep it quiet for now until we can talk to her more?"

"I think so," answered Avery. "Something strange is going on though."

The patio door opened and Mark and Dave were laughing as they walked in. "Hey ladies, did you miss us?" Mark asked.

Dave followed up with, "I believe we are just about ready for the steaks."

Nikki walked out of the bathroom just then. She gave a quick look to the ladies then smiled and grabbed Mark's outstretched arm. He gave her a quick hug and she asked, "You guys got everything under control out on the patio?"

"You betcha!" said Dave.

Avery laughed as she got a fake surprised look on her

face and she said, "Dad, did you just call her a betcha?"

They laughed and that was the first laugh out of Nikki.

Nikki asked, "Do we have time to see Avery's secret garden before dinner?"

"Of course," said Avery, "let me visit the little girls room first." When she finished, she grabbed Nikki's hand and headed out the door.

As they went through the bushes everything was quiet out in the fairy realm. The flowers were only common, there were no specially made by the fairies. This made Marisa say, "These flowers are so beautiful but you were right Avery, I thought there were a lot more colors out here before. Must have been the way the sun was shining on them. Some of them do have that iridescent glow."

"Avery, you were right, this is absolutely heavenly," said Nikki. As she said that a rabbit started to hop into the open but when it saw the people it went the other way and made everyone chuckle a little.

"Now, if we hadn't been here, if only Avery were here" added Dave, "I would bet anything that rabbit would have come right on in."

"I have made a few furry friends out here," answered Avery. "To me it is heaven, Nikki. Inspirational. I love spending time out here."

They made their way back to the house. Avery cornered Marisa before she could join the others and said, "I think we have a problem. I don't think that was a bruise on Nikki's face. It was makeup. More specifically dark eye shadow. I saw some dark powder on the sink and your little eye shadow container was on the shelf, still open. You aren't wearing dark eye shadow, and neither is she, at least not on her eyes. I know you never leave your makeup out like that. Plus, you may have noticed that the bruise was completely gone when she came out of the bathroom the second time, just after we noticed it. She wanted us to think that she covered it up that last time but I believe she wiped it off then."

"What are you saying Avery?" asked Marisa.

"You know exactly what I'm saying," answered Avery. "Come on, we have to go, we can talk about this later."

The men grabbed the steaks to go on the grill and the ladies grabbed all the covered dishes to go on the table. It only took a few minutes for the steaks, so they were all seated and fixing their plates. There was very little talk during the meal, mostly between the ladies, this means either the food is too good for interrupting or talk seemed uncomfortable. In this case it was both.

Part 13

As the plates were emptied Mark said, "Nikki, you have to show them what you brought. They are going to love it. Wait til you see it, it's amazing!"

Nikki volunteered, "Avery, you're going to love this. Mark is right, it's absolutely amazing!"

"Well, let's get these dishes cleared so we can see it!" said Avery.

Marisa chimed in with, "You guys go ahead, I'll get this."

Nikki grabbed her bag and walked back to the island in the kitchen where everyone had gathered. She reached inside the bag and pulled out a glass, domed, display case. She lifted the protective glass dome to introduce a beautiful flower bud. Then she wound a hidden button and the bud opened while *fur elise* played. The flower itself was so good it could have been placed in a vase but it was what was inside that was magnificent. A delicate fairy graced the inside of the flower. It was about three inches tall and maybe four inches wide with its wings fully extended. The body of the fairy was so intricate, and so lifelike, that it appeared as if it could start speaking. The features so delicate and so real.

There were 'ooohs' and 'ahhhhhs' all around as Dave opened a drawer and pulled out a big magnifying glass and brought it over to the figurine. Upon closer examination the inside of the ears were not just plastic and closed up, like on a doll, and the nostrils had actual holes that were so real you expected to feel air come from them. Her eye color was unknown since the tiny eyes were closed, which was a little odd.

There were tiny colored lights flashing to the music and making the fluorescent intricate woven wings almost come to life. Dave, and Avery especially, pored over the sculpture involuntarily muttering things like "beautiful" and "extraordinary." As he went over her head he exclaimed, "I swear you can see where the hair actually comes out of the head, but you can't see the holes like on a doll! This figurine could be alive, it's so real. I mean really, real! Avery are you seeing this?"

Avery pulled out her phone to take a picture while Dave was still going over it with the magnifying glass. Nikki had gone to the sink to help Marisa when Dave said to Avery, "Hey, these wings, they look just like.."

Avery knew he was about to talk about the wings she found and she kicked him lightly on the leg and whispered to him "No, please don't say anything about them, I promise I will explain later."

Nikki said, "What did you say Dave?"

Dave answered, "I was just telling Avery these wings look just like they could start flapping and take off right now. They are woven and intricate and beautiful and so real looking!"

Avery could not stop staring at it. It looked exactly like her friends. She was both amazed and a little scared but she did not know why it frightened her exactly. It was a sculpture, right? "Where did you get this Nikki?" asked Avery.

"I actually found it in my uncle's attic," replied Nikki. "I moved here because of him. He just had some incapacitating surgery so I came to help him. I thought it would be awful, and believe me, he is exhausting, but I love this place." Mark made a throat clearing noise meant to get her attention, and it did. "And of course I met Mark too."

"I'm trying to talk her into staying after he's better," said Mark. "I think it might be working." He looked at Nikki, "At least, I hope it is." Nikki smiled back at him.

The men walked outside to enjoy an after-dinner cigar.

"So, Nikki," asked Avery, "where did your uncle get that gorgeous music box?"

"I don't know. I asked him but then he must have changed the subject because he didn't answer," said Nikki "he was really quiet about it. Almost secretive. After he acted like that, I decided not to take it but then he insisted. I had told him that you like fairies too, but I still don't know anything about it. He started asking questions about you guys, like where you live, and how long you've been here but I thought maybe he was just concerned about me. I don't think so now. Another odd thing was that it was like he wanted me to watch you guys closely as you examined it. I asked why about that too but was again ignored."

"Wow," said Marisa, "that is odd. Maybe it's worth a whole lot of money, it is an amazing work of art."

"I probably shouldn't have told you guys any of that," answered Nikki, "but I have just been so lonely. I've never talked to anyone about this before and I feel like we are friends. Guess I never wanted to share my insanity. I try to give him the benefit of the doubt about his weird ramblings, by thinking maybe this is still some of the drugs from the surgery messing with him. But then again, he wasn't very nice before the surgery, he's worse now."

Marisa looked at Nikki and said, "Well, I know he's your uncle and you're worried about him but maybe you should find your own place and just go in and check on him daily, or better yet, find someone to take care of him."

The look on Nikki's face was enough for Marisa and Avery to ask more questions. They could tell Nikki wanted to talk and Avery was beyond curious as to what she would say next.

Avery's next question was one she believed Nikki was just waiting to answer so she bluntly asked, "Nikki, did you get that bruise from your uncle?" She already knew that it was not a bruise but wondered if Nikki wanted them to believe her uncle was abusive. If so, why?

Marisa said, "Nikki, please don't take this wrong, we do not mean to pry, but if you need to talk about something, please know that we are friends. It looks like you need to talk to someone, and we'd like to get to know you better. You know all about us."

"Well, he's not really my uncle but I have always called him Uncle Jerry," said Nikki, "he was a good friend of my parents. His wife was my dad's distant cousin and when she died he moved into the farmhouse with us and helped with the farm. I remember he was always looking for a get rich quick scheme though. He wasn't serious about farm work. I mean, he worked, but like a lot of people, he wanted to be rich and being a farmer wasn't going to do that. He started several ventures in hopes of hitting it big, and be rich quick, but they failed. With every failure, he seemed to get angrier. And yes, Avery, I'm ashamed to say it but he threw his coffee mug and hit me." She had tears in her eyes as she added, "Please don't tell Mark though, I really want to get this sorted out, and I promise I will leave him, and soon, but Mark doesn't need to be upset about this now."

Marisa and Avery nodded agreement but wondered why she wanted them to believe that he was abusive.

"I was sixteen when my parents were killed in a car accident so that left just him and me. His frustration and anger got worse. Don't get me wrong, he never tried to molest me, never, but he did start throwing things and his bad temper seemed to be escalating. When I was eighteen I left for college. My parents had made sure there were funds for that. He didn't know about that money or I'm sure he would have tried to get it but it was in a trust fund that only I could touch anyway. After I left, he didn't work the farm anymore and just let it go to hell. The farmhouse too. Then finally he left. I don't know where he went or what he did. We didn't keep in touch. Then out of the blue, about three months ago, he called and told me he needed my help. I was living on the East coast and wasn't happy with either my job, or the weather so I agreed to help. Evidently, he made enough money to buy a beautiful house and he has only been in this area for about six months himself. I still don't know what he does though. For some reason I believe that he is involved with some kind of import/export business, but he seems so secretive about it. Maybe I don't want to know, maybe it's not entirely legal and if that's the case then the less I know about it the better."

"Like I said, he was mad when I found the music box but, in my defense, when he abandoned the farm he took everything. I'm sure he sold or pawned anything of value and I'm still mad about that but there's stuff that I might have wanted to keep. Things that were my parents, might be of sentimental value to me. That music box could have originally belonged to my parents."

"Marisa, I want to thank you and Avery for listening to me. Wow, I can't believe I just let it all spill out."

"Are you kidding?" said Marisa. "We are here for you. I know that I speak for Avery as well when I say that I actually feel closer to you now."

"Marisa is right," added Avery, "I think we are going to be the best of friends. Right now though, I am going to excuse myself to get cleaned up and go to bed. It was real nice talking to you Nikki and I hope we see you real soon. Tell Mark and Dad goodnight for me. Goodnight you two." Avery went upstairs to her room, turned on some music, then went to the window to signal Pippa with her flashlight.

Part 14

Avery and the fairies worked out a signal where she turns a flashlight on and sets it in her bedroom window. If any fairies see it, they know that Avery is available for company and may want to talk to them. She knows there is a chance that they are all tucked away for the night and will not see the light and that is okay because they know that if it is an emergency Avery will go to them in person.

It was only a few minutes before Fawn and Pippa flew through the window. Elga was only a few seconds later.

"Is something up, Avery?" asked Fawn.

"Yes, a few things," said Avery, "I just don't know where to start."

Pippa had a concerned look as she quickly glanced at Fawn and Elga before turning her attention to Avery, "Tell us everything."

Just then a creak on the staircase alerted the fairies to run to the bookcase and hide while Avery grabbed her portable keyboard and headphones and threw them on the bed. There was a light rap on the door and Mark asking, "Avery, are you decent?"

Avery put her headphones halfway on her head and answered, "Always Mark, come on in."

"Hey, I didn't get to tell you goodnight, so I thought I'd catch you before you went to bed. Also, I kind of wanted to talk to you a little if that's okay."

"Sure, Mark, what's on your mind?" asked Avery.

"Well, I thought maybe you might have a little more insight than me on something. I have been dating Nikki for a couple months now and everything has been great until just a couple weeks ago. I swear something's going on with Nikki. Something not good and she tells me she's fine and it's nothing for me to worry about but I am. Avery, I'm worried about her."

"Mark, she did talk to me and Marisa about her life, and we were happy that she shared. You probably already know about her parents getting killed and her uncle though, right? I mean she didn't tell us not to tell you so we assumed that you probably already knew."

"Yes, I knew about that but just lately she just seems distant. I really like her and it worries me a little."

"I have to agree with you Mark, she has me a little confused as well. How well do you know Jerry?"

"Not very well, but he's always been polite. I have always been comfortable around him. He's still weak though, sometimes he's even in his wheelchair. He did have open heart surgery so I guess he still isn't completely healed."

"So, he treats Nikki okay though, right? I mean, you don't think he is abusive to her, do you?"

"Oh, God, no! First, he treats her like a princess, and second, he's so weak he couldn't lift a finger to her in anger even if he wanted! Why are you asking about that? What did Nikki tell you?"

Avery could not tell Mark anything about her suspicions just yet because Mark was still in the dark about her fairy friends. She did not think that Nikki was in the dark at all though so she changed the subject matter a little, "She was just telling us about how he let the family home run down and go to hell. I think she is resentful about that."

"I know and that's not good but right now he treats her like his own daughter. You can tell that he thinks the world of her. We've never sat down and had a long conversation, just me and him, but I have talked to him quite a bit over the past few months. I believe that he owned or jointly owned an import/export business. He sold that and made a very good deal. He was able to afford a big, beautiful house in town."

"So, he's not mean to her?"

"Honestly, it's more the other way around. I thought I was falling in love with Nikki until I saw how she treats him. I keep telling myself that she is still mad about the family farm that he lost and how maybe I would feel the same, but I don't think that's it."

"She said that he was initially mad when she found the music box but then he told her it was okay to take it. What's going on with that?" asked Avery.

"From what I understood the other day, he gave that

music box to Nikki but I overheard a part of that conversation and evidently she wanted more than that. I originally thought it meant that he had more music boxes but that wasn't it. It was more like she wanted him to give her a name or a number, some kind of connection that he was not sharing with her. I didn't want to pry so I didn't ask but I didn't notice him acting any differently, except maybe a little quieter, when I picked her up today."

"I don't know Mark," Avery said, "sounds like something strange going on there. If I were you I would take it nice and slow though before you make any major decisions. Know what I mean?"

"Yes, I agree." said Mark. "Funny, I was thinking about taking the next step with her, maybe asking her to move in with me, but I'm glad I waited because I'm not sure how well I like her now. I think she's changed."

Avery got up, hugged Mark and said, "I agree. I know you like her and we like her too, but there's something else going on there."

Mark hugged Avery back, thanked her again, told her goodnight, and started downstairs.

As soon as Mark had descended the stairs, Pippa, Fawn, and Elga flew out of the bookcase and landed on the bed with Avery.

"Sounds like a lot of stuff going on, right?" asked Pippa.

Avery answered, "I've got lots to tell you guys, so get comfortable."

"So much to say, I don't know where to start," said Avery. "First though, let's go back to when I found your wings. Remember me telling you about that?" They all nodded. "Well, what I didn't tell you is that I showed them to my dad. I mean, I knew they were special and I couldn't identify them. My dad is just like me, very curious about nature, and I knew that if he couldn't help me identify them, or research them, nobody could, so I showed him. Okay, now flash forward to today. Nikki brought in this unbelievable music box. So real, it's scary." She pulled out her phone. "I took a picture of it." She brought it up on her phone and held it out for the fairies to see.

As she held her phone for them to see, Pippa screamed as Fawn and Elga both held their little hands over their mouths each also stifling a scream. Avery jumped in surprise and dropped the phone on the bed. The fairies ran to the phone and tried to see the picture again but it was gone. Avery was still shocked by their reaction and tried not to yell as she said, "What the heck was that about? What's going on?"

Pippa quickly said, "Get the picture back, Avery, get it back now!"

"Okay, okay, hold on," Avery answered. She recalled the picture again on her phone and set it on the bed so they could all get as close as they wanted. "I can make it bigger if you need me to."

"Yes, yes!" said Fawn. "Make it bigger, we have to know for sure!"

"Know what?" asked Avery.

"Please, just make it bigger, make the face bigger, please!" cried Pippa.

Avery saw how upset the fairies were so she tried to calm them down a little and said, "Okay, I'm going to enlarge it but you have to calm down and tell me what it is that's upsetting you first."

With tears in her eyes Elga said, "Avery, at first glance we can tell that this is not a doll of any kind. It looks like a real fairy and it looks like a fairy we all knew. We promise to hold it together if you just enlarge the face so we can be sure."

"Of course I will," said Avery. She enlarged the face so that it covered the entire screen. The fairies were all crying as they stared at the picture. "Was this someone you knew?"

"Yes," they said almost in unison.

Pippa said, "This is Everly. She is one of us. She disappeared after the old lady that lived here before went to war with us. We knew she didn't just leave but it was better than thinking she was killed. Who would do such a thing?" She started crying again.

After a full two minutes of the fairies sobbing Elga goes to the picture again. She says "Everly had the most beautiful silver-green eyes but her eyes are almost completely closed in this picture. I wish you could have seen them Avery."

"What do you mean almost completely closed?" asked Avery. "They were completely closed when I looked at them because I questioned that. I wondered out loud why they would not add some beautiful eyes to this beautiful lady. I looked at them. This picture is not what I saw when I was looking at her. They changed from the time I was looking at them to the time I took the picture. One of her eyes is open a little bit more than the other. Not enough to see the actual iris but more than it was when I was looking at them earlier. You can see the white of the eye in this picture. I swear to you. I don't know what that means except that they definitely moved."

"What are you saying Avery?" asked Fern. "Are you sure about that?"

"Yes, I'm absolutely sure," answered Avery. "They moved. I remember seeing them both very tightly closed, I mentioned it out loud. They moved. Does that mean she could possibly be alive somehow? Is there some kind of magic that could make her into a statue like that?"

"Yes," answered Pippa. "We've seen this before. Fairy hunters capture fairies and make a lot of money from them. They use some kind of potion to put the fairies, or whatever they may deem profitable, into a kind of suspended animation. I've heard it can be reversed but we've never had to try it before now. We would have to talk to the elves if this is even the case with Everly. Fairy hunters aren't magic, but they have been around forever and still have access to magic potions.

"Fairy hunters?" asked Avery. "There are actually people who hunt fairies?"

"It's a big business, Avery," added Elga, "Been going on

for many, many years. That's why we have to be so careful. There are collectors, some of us end up on shelves gathering dust."

"How do they find you?" queried Avery.

Pippa looked at the others as she said, "There are several ways, with different indicators, one way is to listen to children. Of course, this is not always reliable because children have very active imaginations. Sometimes though, when they talk of seeing things like fairies or elves, it's worth checking out their stories."

"One of the most reliable ways to find us is to have connections with all the hardware stores or any stores that carry iron. When they find one that has sold a lot of iron they look in the area or maybe they are even lucky enough to get the name of the person who bought it. In this case, the old woman bought a lot of iron but she did it to kill us. There was a lot of activity around here right after she died so we stayed hidden but I'm betting that someone found out about this and came here right after that and got Everly. She wasn't scared of anything. She didn't stay hidden like the rest of us did."

Pippa hung her head, flapped her wings, and sobbed.

Avery interrupted her, "You know I love you guys and I don't mean to sound harsh but first, there's a chance that she can somehow be revived so let's not mourn her death yet. And besides, we don't even have her anyway, we have to figure out a way to get her. But before we do that, there's more I have to tell you."

"Avery's right," said Pippa. "We will get her back. What else do you have to talk to us about Avery?"

Avery sat up straight and said, "So, when we were looking at Everly, just my dad and me, he started to tell me about how the wings looked just like the ones that I found but I stopped him before he could say that out loud. I whispered to him not to mention them and that I would explain later."

"What does that mean Avery?" asked Fern.

"That means that I have to tell Dad about you," Avery said. "I trust him. I know he would be as big an ally to you as I am. He is good to have on our side. I know it's scary for you but you have to trust me on this. He's a friend. I was hoping to introduce you guys tomorrow but of course I need you to agree. If you don't agree then I will have to lie to my dad and tell him some story on why I shushed him when he saw the wings. I will let you decide but then there's even more to what I have to tell you."

Part 15

Pippa, Fern and Elga looked at each other and after just a couple seconds, and no words spoken, they all nodded. Elga said, "We trust you completely Avery, we will meet him tomorrow whenever you wish."

"Thank you," said Avery. "Now, after we examined the music box, I mean Everly, Marisa and I had a little talk with Nikki. You know, she's Mark's girlfriend and she's the one who brought the music box. She opened up to us about her past and her present situation with the man who she calls her uncle." Avery told them Nikki's background and how according to Nikki, at first her uncle was mad when he saw that she had the music box but then he wanted her to show it to us. "According to Nikki, her fake uncle is dangerous and abusive to her. She wants us to believe that he gave her a black eye. After talking to Mark though, I don't think the uncle is bad at all. I don't trust her a bit now. I would bet that she's trying to make him look bad when it's all her. She knows something about the music box and Everly. Why would she specifically watch for my reactions unless she suspects you guys are around here?"

They heard a creaking on the staircase and Pippa, Fawn and Elga all flew to the bookcase.

A light rap on the door and a voice on the other side, "Avery, are you asleep?"

"Come on in Dad," Avery said.

"I think you have something to tell me," Dave said, "what was all that shushing about now?"

Avery looked around her dad at the door and asked, "Where's Marisa?"

"She's gone to bed, I'm alone," he said.

"Close the door, Dad," said Avery.

"Okay, I'm going to tell you something very important, I know that I can trust you with my life and I am now trusting you with other peoples lives, just so you know. Also, this is between only us for now." Her dad raised his eyebrows at this remark and nodded, but before he could speak she continued, "The wings were very special, and they belong to some very special friends of mine. We were going to do this tomorrow but since you're asking now, well, no time like the present. I'm going to introduce you now. Please sit down and don't freak out. Okay, come on out ladies."

At that moment Pippa, Fawn and Elga flew out from the bookcase and landed on the bed with Avery. Dave's eyes got as big as half dollars and his mouth opened wide but nothing came out. He appeared to be paralyzed until Avery snapped him out of it by saying, "Dad, I would like you to meet my friends, Pippa, Fawn and Elga."

"Holy shit, your grandma was right. Your grandma was right!" said Dave in a loud, gravelly, whisper.

Dave was still almost comatose when Elga said, "Because of Avery, and the wings she so carefully collected, I can fly again."

Dave was finally able to whisper, "You're real and you're beautiful. I can't believe you actually exist, but I'm glad. I'm so glad. This explains why Avery spends all her time out back and I don't blame her."

"Dad, what did you mean?" asked Avery. "What did you mean when you said my grandma was right?"

"Your mom grew up believing in fairies because of your grandma." answered Dave. "Then when we were married, she told me the same stories. They were so believable too.

She told us of how she played with fairies and elves when she was a little girl. They protected her. They were her friends. She had too many stories for them not to be true. You were young when she passed away, but she was the one that named you."

Avery had tears in her eyes when she said, "I wish I had known her."

Dave shook his head as if to clear away the memories. Avery got back to the moment too and said, "All the flowers and the beauty in the back are there because of the fairies and elves."

"Elves too?" asked Dave. "I can't wait to meet more and please trust me that I will not betray you, but I have so many questions."

"In good time Dad, but right now we have a more pressing issue," said Avery. "The music box that Nikki brought is more than just an expensive item." She told her dad about Everly, the eyelids closing, and the suspicion of some kind of suspended animation in play.

"Oh shit!" Dave said. "We have to do something. We have to fix this. I'm so sorry that I'm staring, it's just that you ladies are nothing less than magnificent!"

"Well, thank you dear," said Pippa. "May we call you Dave?"

"Yes, please, of course," answered Dave.

"Dad, I have already told these ladies more about Nikki and her fake uncle." said Avery. "I know that she told Marisa and me some things in confidence but if we're going to ask you to help us, I think you need to know too." She told her dad what Nikki had told her and Marisa. Then she told him about her conversation with Mark. "I believe, and the ladies agree, that Nikki has some ulterior motives. You know how I feel about Mark, but I don't think Nikki is in it just for him. Before I talked to Mark, I thought that it was Nikki's fake uncle but now I know it isn't him at all. It's all Nikki. Her fake uncle was never abusive to her. That bruise she had was from eye shadow, she faked it. I went to the bathroom right after her and I noticed that one of Marisa's dark eye shadow containers was not put away and Marisa never leaves her stuff out. Also, if there had been a real bruise Mark would have noticed it too. I'm convinced that she suspects fairies in the area and Everly is the bait."

"I know we have lots more to talk about, but you better go to bed before Marisa gets suspicious and starts looking for you. We can talk tomorrow."

"Yes," said Dave, "We'll have all day. Marisa is going shopping with Nikki in the morning then they are going to lunch, I was going to go to the office but there's no way I'd be concentrating on work, I'm yours all day. I'm anxious to see it alive in the back. I don't know if I'll be able to sleep. Good night, Avery. Good night you gorgeous ladies, and I want to thank all of you for trusting me."

After Dave walked out Pippa, Fawn and Elga started talking all at once. Avery had to hold out her hands and say, "Stop, stop, stop, I can't understand any of you when you're all talking together." When there was a silence she asked, "So, how do you feel about revealing yourselves? Were we wrong to do that? I mean, I know we can trust my dad but how do you feel about it? Are you upset?"

"No, no, we are not upset," said Pippa. "I think we are happy! We trust you and we trust Dave and we have never, never been able to say that about any humans! I know that there are many groups that have human friends, but we've never been able to say that, until you. You've restored a little faith in humankind for us and we thank you for that. Tomorrow, I think we will share more with you and your dad. It will be exciting for all of us." The fairies flew to the window and bid Avery goodnight.

Part 16

The next morning started with the promise of a beautiful day. The sun was shining, the birds were singing, and there was a pleasant breeze moving the flowers almost as if to music. Dave and Avery watched Marisa drive away then promptly headed for the back. As they passed by the hedges that separated the immediate back yard from the paradise the fairies called home, Avery told her dad, "There are always elves working around these bushes and ready to send an alarm if intruders pass. You can't see them but they are here, so I always wish them a good morning. Good morning little angels, lots of excitement back here today!" A couple elves appeared on the top of a bush and waved hello to Avery.

Dave was still so awestruck, he smiled and kept repeating, "Amazing, everything here is amazing."

They stopped at the center tree where Pippa, Fawn and Elga were perched. Fawn said, "We've had a meeting and all are in agreement that we will show you around. Avery, you've been with us for a while now, but you have yet to see the other part of our world."

"What? What are you talking about?" asked Avery.

Pippa smiled and said, "You and Dave are in for a treat. You may be the only humans to ever visit a real fairy kingdom. You have proved to us that you are trustworthy so we are going to open our doors for you."

"Where is your kingdom? I thought we were standing in it," asked Dave.

"Well, you are," answered Pippa, "but there's much, much more. First you both have to trust us to fix you so that you are compatible to our other world. We need to sprinkle a little fairy dust on you. It doesn't hurt. There's a little hole right here at the root of this tree. After your size adjustment you will enter the hole and slide down the tube, the shooter. Meet Twill and Mackie," she pointed to two elves standing by the hole and they nodded to Avery and Dave, "they will escort you through the shooter to make sure you do not go too fast, it might be a little scary for you at first. Are you game?"

"Absolutely!" cried Avery.

"Absolutely!" repeated Dave.

Fawn and Elga flew above Avery and Dave and sprinkled what looked like diamond dust on them. It sparkled beautiful colors in the sunlight and as Avery watched it she noticed she was shrinking. She looked at her dad and he was shrinking as well. They reached out to each other and held hands as they shrunk to approximately three inches in height. Twill and Mackie came over to them and led them to the hole. Twill sat down and instructed Avery to sit right behind him, followed by Dave, then Mackie at the end. As they inched forward in the once tiny hole they began to slide downward. The slide was designed in a circular fashion to take up less room for going a greater distance underground and so that it would not be such a drastic drop.

When they finally landed, Avery and Dave felt like they had traveled miles but when they remembered their size, they realized it just seemed like miles. Twill and Mackie helped them out of the shooter and they were both awestruck at their surroundings. They were in a whole new world. It was huge and bright but not from the sun. On the ceiling there were tiny things that resembled stars, thousands of them, maybe millions. It lit up the area like the sun. They could not believe what they were seeing. It was a city. There were shops and houses and people milling all around. Most of the people, or fairies, stopped and surrounded them. They had all heard about Avery but only a dozen or so had actually met her and they had been told about her dad, Dave. They were satisfied that they were both trustworthy, so they welcomed them. They were all beautiful beings. Avery could not help but refer to them as people because she was the same size now. She knew they were fairies or elves, or maybe even elflings. She had so much to learn about them.

When Pippa, Fawn and Elga appeared, Avery could not help herself. She hugged them all and said, "I'm so happy that I can hug you now."

Dave was still in awe as he looked all around. He saw

huge butterflies flitting about and he pointed at them. When he realized they were not giant but that he was tiny he became a little alarmed. Pippa put her hand on his shoulder and said, "I see you are admiring the flutterbys. Don't worry, everything down here is friendly, and everyone has been told to expect you and Avery. A lot of them have already met Avery."

"I'm so glad that you confided in me," said Dave. "This is absolutely amazing."

Pippa took both their hands and pulled them through the crowd. She got in the middle, stopped, turned around and said, "Everyone, this is Avery and her dad, Dave. I don't know if Avery is aware of this, but we all know that the name Avery means *wise ruler of fairies and elves*. We also all know that she has proved to be a trustworthy friend. We owe her our lives. That her name just happens to be Avery is, I believe to be more than just a happy coincidence."

Avery snapped her head around to look at Pippa and said, "I know that you told me that before but I had always thought that it meant wise but I like your definition much better."

"Ah yes, but so much more," added Pippa, "I knew when you first told me your name that we had a good friend in you. I know that humans have sometimes two or more names aside from their surnames, do you have another one?"

Avery bowed her head slightly as she said, "Yes, I have a middle name. It is Guinevere."

A small gasp fell among the crowd, followed by cheering. Avery looked at Pippa, "What did I say?"

"You said that you were a white fairy. That's the meaning of the name Guinevere," answered Pippa.

"I guess I really do fit in here then," said Avery. "Did you know that Dad?"

"Yes," said Dave. "Your mom and I were hopeless romantics and wanted so badly to believe in fairies but as adults, we were realistic enough to know that our dream would have to be just that, a dream." His eyes filled with tears and he choked on the words as he said, "She would have loved this."

"I'm sorry Dave, I wish she were here too," said Pippa. "Let me show you around. We are in one of our gathering places. We have many of these. Hundreds of our folk can gather here comfortably. This one is under one of our old Hawthorn trees."

Part 17

The place where they stood was like a village itself. There were little areas that reminded Avery of little farmer's stands where people sold their fruits or vegetables. Nothing was for sale there though, people traded instead. There were flowers and reeds, seeds and vines, honey and nectars. There was some kind of drink too. Someone handed them a little cup of drink and they accepted, but before Avery could take a drink Pippa stopped her. "Avery, no. You can't have that. It's not good for children and it would make you sick. Dave, you can drink it though." Pippa drank it herself, handed Avery a different cup and said, "This you can have though. It's not fermented like the other."

Dave drank it and said, "Wow, that's delicious but I can tell it's potent."

"We do like our cider here. We make a variety of drinks, some that are without effects, like the one Avery had, and many with divine effects. I believe you may have to work your way up to our absinthe, Dave. It's delicious, as they all are, but extremely potent. Most humans do not have our tolerance."

Avery knew that it was alcohol and she was too young, but the fairies liked alcohol and drank it daily. The great room was full of fairies going about their business. Some were creating things, others were tending to plants or animals. The roots of the hawthorn tree were all around but they were also well cared for by the fairies. Pippa told Avery that in exchange for giving them this underground world, the fairies and elves fed and nourished any of the root system that was exposed.

Squirrels and chipmunks, many with riders, darted around the big room. There were other small creatures that Avery could not identify but they all roamed freely and peacefully. Even the creatures seemed to have jobs. It was hard for her to remember that she was only maybe three inches tall because everyone was about her size or even smaller. She remembered quickly though when she saw that squirrels and chipmunks were larger than her. It did not scare her though. Everything was peaceful and busy.

Rabbits hopped about freely and without fear. One stopped right near Dave and he reached out to pet it. "Would you like to ride a bunny?" asked Pippa.

"I would never have imagined someone asking me that," laughed Dave, "but yes, that would be insane!"

Pippa looked at Avery and said, "Don't worry Avery, I have something else for you to hop on, we'll see it in a few minutes." Avery's eyes got real wide as she nodded. Pippa reached her hand out to the bunny and the bunny laid down so that Dave could climb on behind its head. The bunny rose then, and Pippa told Dave to hang on. It hopped very slowly around in a little circle while Avery, Pippa, and the others all laughed at Dave's expressions. Pippa reached out her hand again and the bunny came over to her so Dave could dismount. He looked just like a little kid when he said, "That was so amazing!"

"It would take days for you two to explore our world," said Pippa, "and you can always come back but there's just something you should see. It's the reason I brought you here so let's continue."

They walked through another corridor into another large area. "Avery, this is the area I think you will love," said Pippa. Avery noticed something resembling a dog walking toward a very bright hall. It was bigger than a great dane, at least compared to her current size. As it got closer to the bright light she noticed it was even bigger than she had originally thought, it was not a dog at all, it was a horse! Then something incredible happened. Its wings unfolded and it took flight.

Pippa saw what Avery was staring at and said, "That's a horsefly."

"No," Avery said, "It's a pegasus, and it's magnificent! I didn't think they ever really existed, did they actually exist?"

Pippa looked at her and answered, "Yes, they existed in your world many, many years ago but man would have killed them all so we enchanted some to a smaller size to save them. We brought them to our underground world and they have thrived but we know that if we re-introduce them to your world, they will again be hunted and killed or at the very least unable to live in peace. We have everything here for them that they need to thrive, even meadows under the sun. We have many other animals that exist and thrive here that no longer exist in your world. You will see."

Fawn reached out her hand and a horsefly came over. She looked at Avery and said, "Are you ready for a ride, Avery?"

Avery had tears in her eyes and she was so choked up you could barely make out her answer, "Yes, yes, please, yes!"

"I think that means she's ready," said Dave laughing.

Avery looked at the horsefly and said, "You are the most beautiful, magnificent, creature I have ever seen! What is your name please?"

Fawn said, "This is Xander. Xander meet Avery." Xander put one front leg out and bowed his head to Avery in greeting.

Avery could not contain her excitement as she curtsied in response to Xander's bow, and said, "It is beyond my pleasure to meet you Xander!" Xander stayed in a somewhat prone position so Avery could climb onto his back. Dave snapped a picture, although he knew the pictures they took would be only seen by them. Dave riding a white bunny and Avery riding a shiny black pegasus, these could easily be explained by a visit to one of the big theme parks that feature wild rides such as this, but they knew the truth.

Avery was talking to Xander as he gently flew off. Moments later Xander gently landed right where he had started and Avery dismounted. She hugged Xander's neck fiercely and said, "Thank you Xander. I love you." Xander pawed the ground in response. Then she looked at the ladies and said, "And I want to thank you for this, and I love you all too!"

Surrounding this gathering place were what looked like huge, ornate archways leading into tunnels all around. They were headed for the one where Xander went. It was even much brighter than the gathering room itself. Pippa took Avery's hand and said, "I thought you would be interested in this. You were so excited about the horsefly."

Fawn laughed and said, "I can't wait until she meets our dragonflies!"

"What?" asked Avery.

"Another day, Avery," said Pippa. "We have something more pressing right now."

Fawn took Dave's hand and they followed. Dave was definitely feeling the effects of the drink but it was not what he would call a drunk effect, it was like he was more aware, and alive. It was good. He was happy.

They walked into a short tunnel and out in the bright sunlight on a huge meadow. In the meadow were hundreds of horseflies either milling about on the ground or flying around in the air. All colors from solid black to solid white and everything in between, even what looked like paint horses. Avery looked shocked as she asked Pippa, "How can you be out in the open like this? And how is it I have never seen them before? This has to be on our land, right?"

Pippa smiled and said, "This is one of our many meadows and yes it is out in the open but humans can't see them. They are covered with an enchantment, a dome that keeps us hidden from human eyes. But, if there is any danger of someone accidentally walking through them, the entire area is automatically dropped below the earth. At least temporarily. We always make our meadows out where there are very few humans. All of the meadows in this realm have been here for many, many years, without incident."

"Wow," said Avery, "These horseflies are amazing, everything is amazing. I feel like I am in heaven, or at least a whole new world."

"You are in a different world, Avery," said Pippa, "You are in a fairy realm. Humans rarely see this world. We have to be careful, as you know, only a handful of humans could say they have seen this but of course they don't. We only allow faithful humans to see our worlds."

Pippa talked a little more about the meadows, but she told Avery and Dave that this was only a tiny part of their world, but they should continue. It would take days to see everything. They both wanted to linger here, it was so beautiful, but they also figured that beauty was going to be around every corner, so they followed Pippa.

Down another corridor from the gathering place they walked a short distance and stopped at another great root system. Avery knew they were under another tree. Before they could go any farther, Elga flew up to them with four other fairies. She looked at Avery with tears in her eyes and said, "Avery, these are the other fairies that have been mended because you took such good care of our wings. We can't thank you enough." They were all voicing their 'thanks' together. It almost sounded like glorious singing voices in harmony. It was beautiful.

"It was definitely my pleasure," said Avery. "I'm so happy that you are all mended."

Part 18

Pippa led Avery and Dave over to the wall where there were

hundreds, maybe thousands of framed prints of some kind. She pointed to one in particular and asked Avery to take out her phone. "These are similar to the photographs that you have but these are made by our elves. I wanted you to see this one specifically."

As soon as Avery took a closer look she knew why Pippa had asked her to take out her phone. It was the exact likeness of the music box fairy that Nikki had brought over. Avery brought the picture up on her phone and held it to the one on the wall. They were identical.

Pippa looked at them and said, "This is why I brought you here. That music box, that miserable thing that is no more than a toy now, is one of our sister fairies, Everly."

"Oh my God," whispered Avery, "Dad, look at this."

Dave's eyes widened when he saw the comparison, "How is this possible? What can we do?"

"I don't know yet," replied Pippa, "but let's get you home for now, then we'll make some kind of plan." Pippa instructed Dave and Avery to stand on a little platform and when they did, it began to rise. Fawn and Elga flitted alongside as the platform raised them to a hole in the tree. They exited it onto a branch high up in the tree. Fawn held Avery while Elga held Dave and they floated gently down to the ground where Pippa was waiting. As soon as they went a little distance from the tree Pippa flew above them and sprinkled some fairy dust over them. It was only a matter of seconds before they were back to their normal human size. "I had to make sure the area was secure before we changed you back."

Dave and Avery sat down on the ground. They both felt exhausted, yet exhilarated, from their journey and they knew they would want to go back. They realized they had just experienced something that very few humans had seen. They also knew that humans had wronged them, and they needed to help, but they had no idea how they were going to do that. Pippa landed on Dave's lap while Fawn and Elga went to Avery's. Elga was the first to break the silence. "So you can see that we need to rescue Everly, and we are going to need your help. We need some kind of plan."

"So, you believe that she is somehow still alive?" asked Dave.

"Yes," answered Pippa. "She is in some form of suspended animation. She is in there, she entrusted Avery, even in her present form, she was trying to blink a message to a trustworthy person and she chose Avery. Avery is the only one who caught that, and those people have had her for months. We must get her back here, somehow."

Dave looked up at the house and said, "I better go back to the house in case Marisa comes home, but we'll think of something won't we Avery?"

"We have to," said Avery. "I'll go back to the house with you, but I'll be back later."

The fairies watched them walk back and Fawn said, "I know they'll help us. They'll figure out a way to get her back and keep us safe."

As they walked back to the house, Avery and Dave both felt as if they had a huge weight on their shoulders. "I have never felt like this before," said Dave. "I mean this is the most important thing that has ever happened to me, and it's like you and I have the weight of the world on our shoulders right now. Is that how you feel?"

Avery stopped and looked at Dave, "Dad, I agree. This is a real life and death situation, and I have no idea right now how we are going to handle it."

"Yep," replied Dave. "As stupid as I feel right now though, I have faith that between the two of us, and of course the fairies, we will find a way to fix this. We have to. We can't fail this one."

They looked at each other, hugged, then silently walked back to the house.

Avery and her dad were in the kitchen. Dave could still feel the effects of the drink from the fairies when he poured some tea for him and Avery. He said, "Wow, that is some potent stuff, I'm sure you could get hammered on that stuff real quick. I'm certainly not an alcohol connoisseur but it seems different than our normal stuff. I felt happy but not drunk happy. Hard to explain but one more drink and I think it would have kicked my happy ass. I can't believe they drink that all the time."

Avery said, "I know what I drank wasn't alcohol but it had some kind of effect on me as well. Not what I would imagine being drunk, but more like happy, I can't explain it."

"Yeah, that's what it was more like, it made me feel just really good," added Dave. "We need to get some more of that!"

"Okay, now, before Marisa gets home," said Avery, "we need some kind of plan."

Dave looked around the room like he was looking for an answer, anywhere, and finally said, "We need to get Everly back here so the elves can bring her back to life. How are we going to do that?"

"Occam's razor," said Avery. "You taught me that. Look for the simplest solution. Simple in this case would be that you offer to buy it for me, as a surprise. I don't think that she's going to go for that but if she doesn't, maybe we could at least ask her if she would bring it back. She knows I'm a kid that loves all kinds of fairies and nature and stuff. I'll ask her if she can bring it back again so I can take pictures of it. Pictures of it up in my room, surrounded by other fairies and unicorns and supernatural stuff. If she agrees, I will have all the necessary things in my room, including the elves. You and Marisa will need to keep her occupied down here. We'll have to see if the elves can put something in Everly's place though, but I bet if they can reanimate her then surely, they can magically replace her with something. What do you think?"

"That doesn't sound like a very viable reason to get her in your room," said Dave. "Maybe I can offer her enough to buy her. That would solve everything. Avery, I'm not embarrassed to say it, but I'm scared, this is a very important task we have been given."

Dave heard a car in the driveway and said, "One thing I have noticed though is that we have to stop referring to the music box as 'her.' It is simply a beautiful music box. It is a music box."

About that time Marisa and Nikki walked in the house.

Part 19

"Anyone home?" called Marisa.

"In the kitchen," Dave yelled. As they walked into the kitchen he added, "Hello ladies, so did you buy out the stores?"

"We tried," chuckled Marisa.

"She tried," laughed Nikki, "I bought one little thing, but this lady knows how to shop! I'm exhausted but I think it just pepped her up!"

"Ooooh, what did you get Marisa?" asked Avery.

"Lets go in the other room and I'll show you!" said Marisa.

Avery and Marisa left the kitchen. Dave looked at Nikki and said, Speaking of shopping, can I ask you for something important, Nikki?"

"Sure, what can I do for you Dave?" answered Nikki.

"Well, I don't think you know just how much Avery fell in love with your music box," said Dave. "Her birthday is coming up and I was wondering if you would possibly sell it to me. I've looked online and some of those music boxes and statues are pretty pricey so I'm willing to pay you a good price. What do you say? It would make her so happy. Will you sell it to me? I'm rambling now, so please answer me before it gets worse."

Nikki smiled, "I'm not even sure that it's mine to sell, it may be Uncle Jerry's. I know he took everything of value from my parents' farmhouse, but I don't know who that really belongs to."

"Please," added Dave. "It would be the best surprise

ever!"

Nikki looked at Dave and said, "I'll talk to him, but I can't promise anything. He's still on some heavy medication."

"That's all I can ask for, except, well, if you decide you can't sell it to me could you at least bring it out again so Avery can take some pictures of it?" asked Dave.

Nikki answered, "I'm pretty sure I could at least do that, but I'll talk to Uncle Jerry when I get home and let you know, okay?"

Dave nodded a thank you to Nikki.

Marisa and Avery walked back into the kitchen. Marisa looked at Nikki and said, "We can have a little barbecue tonight if you and Mark would like to come, we have all the fixings for one."

"That sounds good, I'll run it by Mark but if I know him, he's not going to turn down a barbeque!" laughed Nikki.

"Good then," said Marisa, "guess we'll see you tonight."

Nikki said goodbye to everyone and walked out.

"Thank you again, Marisa," said Avery, "they're beautiful! Dad look what Marisa got me."

Avery was pointing to her ears. Dave looked and his eyebrows shot up a little as he said, "Those are absolutely stunning earrings! They are so delicate and beautiful. Fairies, right?"

"Yep," said Avery, "they are beautiful. I love them."

"You are very welcome," answered Marisa, "I saw them and I had to get them. They practically screamed out your name."

Avery said, "Well, I'm gonna go out back and sing to the trees, Dad would you like to join me?"

Dave looked at Marisa and said, "I think I would, Marisa would you like to go too?"

Marisa was digging in the refrigerator as she said, "No thank you, I better get the stuff ready for the barbeque. The singing sounds more fun though, can I take a rain check?"

"You certainly can, our next concert will most likely be

tomorrow, would you like it if I got you tickets?" asked Avery.

"Please, yes," laughed Marisa.

Part 20

Avery and Dave walked out back. This time Dave looked at the hedges as they entered the back 'realm' and there on the top were Twill and Mackie, two of the elves he had previously met. Dave and Avery both said hello to them and they waved their acknowledgement.

Although Avery was still amazed at the goings-on in the back, she had gotten a little past the starstruck phase every time she walked back there. Her dad was still in the starstruck phase. As he looked around, he stared at every little magical thing. If someone wanted his attention, they would most likely have to ask him twice, he was so enthralled by his surroundings.

About five fairies were flying around the flowers when they saw Dave and Avery. They flew up to them and landed on their shoulders. Avery's dad looked like a little kid the way he still looked at them in awe. Soon they were surrounded by fairies and elves, all waiting to hear what they had to say. Avery and her dad sat down on a little bench nestled inside a beautiful flower bed. Then, within moments, there were dozens of tiny, beautiful people. Non-flying elves were climbing up on bench to get closer to the humans. Dave held down his hand for a couple elves to jump in and he lifted them to his lap. It was clear he was very comfortable and happy in their company.

Pippa, Fawn, and Elga flew up and landed on Dave's lap. Pippa said, "Well, Dave, as you can see we are all so anxious to see what you are thinking and of course what we need to do."

Dave looked around at all the tiny, beautiful, hopeful, faces and smiled. He looked at Avery as he began, "Avery and I have a couple theories on how to handle this. The first one, and the simplest, would be if I could possibly buy the music box imprisoning Everly. Remember, we are not supposed to know that there is a real person inside the music box, so we have to treat it as an expensive object when talking to Nikki. It's very hard for us now to do that, but we must."

"We understand Dave," said an elf on his lap, "and we all want you to know that whatever you do, we appreciate it, even if the results are not what we want."

"Oh, no," Dave answered quickly, "we will get the desired results. I am, or I should say we are, very determined now. Right Avery?"

Avery nodded and said, "So Dad has already offered a lot of money for the music box but Nikki told him that she would have to check with her uncle before she could give him an answer. Neither one of us believe that is true. We believe she is in control so we don't know what she's got in mind. It's a little daunting."

Dave took over then and said, "So, then I asked if she could at least bring it over again so that Avery could take pictures of it. Nikki didn't know that Avery had already snuck a picture of it. She casually said that she guessed she could do that."

Avery jumped in with, "That's where you guys come in. If she brings Everly with her tonight, I will take her up to my room where you guys will be waiting to work your magic. I will leave the window open for fairies but Dad and I will give anyone else a ride. You need to make sure that you have everything you will need and we will get you up to my room before Nikki comes tonight, just in case she does bring Everly. If she doesn't bring Everly and decides she won't sell the music box I don't know what we will do."

"I do," said Dave. "We will steal her."

Avery looked at her dad with a very shocked expression and said, "Dad, we didn't discuss that option at all."

"I know," answered Dave, "But I have a bad feeling about Nikki going along with a sale, no matter how much I offer. She has something else in mind. I think she is looking for more of our magical friends and I won't let that happen. We can't let that happen."

"I agree," said Avery, "But we all know that stealing wouldn't make her stop. It would only make her more apt to come after us. We have to think about taking care of Nikki. I can't believe I said that out loud."

"You did," said Pippa, "We appreciate and love you guys for preparing to do what needs to be done but we can't let you do something you might be sorry for later. Remember I told you that we are not helpless. Alone, with no human friends, we can be hurt terribly, maybe even decimated, like we were when the previous owners were here, but with you and Dave we are a very strong army. We will be the ones to do any dirty work that needs to be done. We are normally a very loving, caring, community until it comes to people with nefarious purposes, then we can be downright wicked. We protect our own, and you and Dave are our own, now."

"Okay," said Dave, "Mark and Nikki will be over tonight for dinner so Avery and I will come back in a couple hours. We can carry everything you need, including any non-flying people up to Avery's room. Other than that, I guess we just have to wait and see. It's Nikki's move now."

Avery looked around and said, "I'll come back before they get here with a basket to collect flowers and whoever wants to come to the house can just get on board with the flowers then."

Part 21

Mark parked the car and walked to the door. He could hear shouting inside between Nikki and Jerry. He opened the door but did not go all the way inside yet. He felt uneasy eavesdropping but he was more curious than ever because of what he was hearing. Jerry seemed to be upset as he was explaining something to Nikki. He was talking fast as he told his story.

"Nikki, I came here following a lead about some iron bought from the store in town. I lied to those who sent me when I reported that the iron bought here was bought by someone in another town over 200 miles away. I told them I was no longer interested in chasing imaginary fairy tales. But that was a lie. I didn't think it was a fairy tale anymore. That music box was real, at least at one time it was. I believed that. I couldn't fix that but I could maybe protect other innocent beings out there by telling those people there was nothing here. I did research. I knew there were other hunters out there but at least maybe I could keep them away from this area. I told them I accidentally broke the music box. They were pretty mad about that but I sent them some money to cover it and told them I was done. Nothing here. They believe it is a dead end here. I told them goodbye and changed my telephone number. A week later I was in the hospital having heart surgery, that's when I called you."

"No, no, no," whispered Nikki. Then her voice got louder and louder, "That's not good enough. Do you think I'm gonna work in a shitty dress shop for minimum wage when I can be rich? You're going to call those people or give me their information and I'll call."

"No, Nikki, those people are bad." Jerry pleaded. "I watched them kill someone and didn't give it a second thought. I thought I was bad until I met them. I have severed myself from them and I'll never see them again. I'm lucky I got out of it alive. They must never find out where we are."

Nikki's voice had raised to a yell as she said, "Oh yes they will find out where we are, and I will tell them. We have something they want. I know that little Avery bitch knows something and I'm going to find out. She's hiding something and I think it's something those people would love to know about. I think her smartass Dad may know too. I don't think Marisa has a clue though, she's a true dumbass. I'm going to be rich, and if I have to hurt a few people to do it, I don't give a goddamn. They're nobody and nothing to me except standing in my way of money."

That was all Mark needed to hear to rush down the hall to the kitchen. Before he hit the doorway there was a loud crash. He hurried inside just in time to see Jerry wiping blood from his cheekbone. An electric can opener, thrown by Nikki, had hit him squarely on the side of his face. He was slumped over in his wheelchair trying to talk to Nikki when Mark appeared in the doorway. "What the hell's going on in here?" he asked. He ran over to Jerry and grabbed a towel to help him stop the bleeding. "Nikki? What's wrong with you? He's hurt!"

"Come on in Mark, join the party." said Nikki. "Oh yeah, we have a barbeque to attend, don't we?"

"Get out of here while you can," said Jerry. "Get as far away from Nikki as you can. I mean it."

"Nope," replied Nikki, "I think you need to be here, Mark. After all, it's your friends we're talking about. They're hiding something and I'm going to get it. Uncle Jerry here is turned into a bit of a pussy about this shit so I guess it's all on me."

"What's going on? What are you talking about?" asked Mark.

"Well," chuckled Nikki, "it seems your friends have a big secret. A big lucrative secret. Right there on their land. They have some creatures living out there that some people will pay a lot of money for. Only problem is Jerry, the pussy over there, won't give me his contact so I can talk to these people, but don't worry, I'll get it from him, one way or another." She pulled out a gun and pointed it at Jerry.

"Nikki, please," cried Jerry, "you would be hurting innocent, living, beings. I know you're not like that."

Mark looked at Nikki and the gun with surprise and said, "I won't let you hurt Jerry or my friends!"

The gun fired as Nikki said, "Shut up Mark." The noise was deafening as Mark hit the wall and crumpled to the floor bleeding. Then she redirected the gun to Jerry and said, "I'll turn this place upside down and I'll find a connection. Don't think I need you anymore so fuck you Uncle Jerry." She fired the gun and a tiny red hole appeared in Jerry's forehead as he slumped over in his wheelchair. "Guess I have a barbeque to attend. Oh, yeah, I don't want to forget the guest of honor." Gun in hand, she grabbed the music box and headed toward the door.

Part 22

Avery walked into the kitchen and asked Marisa, "Is there anything I can do to help you, Marisa?"

"I've got it covered, sweetie, but thank you," answered Marisa.

"Then I'm gonna go get some fresh flowers for the table," Avery said. She grabbed a basket and went out the back door. When she got to the back property she put the basket on the ground and said with a chuckle, "All aboard, that's coming aboard. The basket will be leaving the station shortly." She took the clippers from the basket, cut several flowers, and placed them in the basket while the elves were climbing in. The elves hid under the flowers for their first trip to the human house. When Avery entered the house, she slipped by the kitchen and went upstairs first to drop the elves off and make sure the window was open. Then she took the flowers to the kitchen and arranged them in a vase.

"Those are beautiful, Avery," said Marisa, "You really have an eye for decorating!"

"Thank you me lady," Avery answered in a cockney accent that caused them both to laugh.

Dave headed out to the patio to prepare the grill when he heard the doorbell. He looked at Marisa quizzically and said, "That must not be Mark, he doesn't ring the bell anymore, he just walks in." Nikki stood alone on the other side of the door as Dave opened it. "Hey Nikki, you don't have to be so formal, Mark just walks right in. Where is Mark?"

"He'll be along shortly," said Nikki, "He said there was something at the store that he needed to do so for me to go ahead without him, so here I am. I brought the music box and I decided I would sell it to you."

"That's great, Nikki!" said Dave. "Avery will be so excited. Let me pay you for it first and then I want to take it upstairs and surprise Avery." He led Nikki into the study where he had the cash ready. "I was very hopeful that you would decide to sell it so I had this all ready, just in case. This is $6,000 is that what we agreed on?"

"I would like to go with you when you surprise Avery, is that okay?" asked Nikki.

Marisa heard voices and yelled out, "Dave, is that Mark and Nikki?"

Dave answered with, "Mark isn't here yet but Nikki and I are going upstairs to see Avery real quick. We'll be right back."

As they neared the top step Dave yelled out, "Avery, Nikki and I are bringing you a surprise."

Avery shouted for everyone to hide because Dave was not alone. The fairies flew up into the bookcase while the elves hid among the pillows on the bed. Dave came through the door first. Nikki stood in the doorway holding the music box in her left hand and a gun in her right. Avery saw the gun and screamed. Before Dave could turn completely around Nikki hit him in the back of the head with the gun. He fell to the floor.

Downstairs Marisa heard Avery's scream followed by a loud thud and she ran up the stairs. She was running so hard she almost ran into Nikki who was just inside the threshold of Avery's room. Nikki turned to face Marisa and said, "Ah, Marisa, so happy you could join us."

Marisa looked at Dave on the floor and the gun in Nikki's hand. She saw the scared expression on Avery's face as she was running over to check on Dave. Even with a gun held on her, Marisa was not deterred. She yelled "You don't fuck with my family!" She hauled off and punched Nikki square in the face. It was a very well executed punch but Nikki was prepared and she did not completely lose her balance. One second later she was recovered enough to punch Marisa in the face with the gun in her hand. Marisa went down immediately, bleeding profusely.

This few seconds of commotion was all the distraction Pippa and Fawn needed to fly above Nikki and sprinkle some dust down on her. Avery grabbed the music box as Nikki immediately started shrinking. When she was down to three inches a couple of elves hurried over to her with an upside down drinking glass, and set it on top of her, trapping her.

Part 23

Avery was crying as she checked on her dad. He was unconscious and his head was still bleeding. She choked out the words, "My dad is hurt and so is Marisa, I have to call 911." Pippa stopped her before she could grab her phone.

Several fairies were fluttering above Dave's head, while elves stood on the back of his neck doing their healing magic. Pippa said, "Avery, you know I told you before that we can help humans and that's what we're doing now." Dave started to push himself from the floor. His head was no longer bleeding. It was as if nothing had happened to him. He saw Avery's tears and grabbed her. They hugged each other hard. Dave looked in the hallway and saw Marisa laying there with blood all around her. Fairies danced above her, sprinkling dust while elves healed her from the ground. She opened her eyes.

Epilogue

They heard the sirens first. Moments later a knock on the door and a voice announcing it was the police. They told Dave they had received a 911 call from Mark. He told them someone with a gun was coming here. Mark was now in emergency surgery for a gunshot wound.

Dave surrendered the gun that Nikki had brought with intentions of robbing them but they had luckily overpowered her. In the struggle she lost her gun and her car keys, and was forced to flee on foot. Dave had wiped any traces of blood from the gun, since none of the victims were injured. The gun and her car were immediately impounded by the police and a BOLO was put out on Nikki. They would never find her.

In the underground fairy realm they had created a special chamber for their new guest. In the wall were niches with the newest addition already in place. It was a beautiful flower music box. The flower opened to reveal a lovely lady holding a tiny gun, and if you looked very closely at her eyes you would see movement there. There were other niches for possible future guests.

One week later Dave, Marisa, Avery and Mark had a celebratory barbeque.

The table was set with both human size dinnerware and miniature size dinnerware. Miniature plates, bowls, cups and silverware. The human size dinnerware was placed two on each side, the miniature dinnerware was scattered between and around them. There was no separation because of size.

Fawn flutters over, lands on Marisa's shoulder, and says, "Marisa, the table is lovely. Thank you so much for inviting us."

Marisa says, "No invitations necessary here Fawn. This is just the start of our new family meals. You are family. I wish I could hug you!"

Fawn laughed and said, "Oh, that'll happen! But for now, I can feel your hug and I'm hugging you back!"

Everyone was gathered around, or on, the table when Everly said, "I know that I owe my life to each and every one of you here. Words are not enough but thank you." She was choked up enough that she could not continue with words. Her beautiful silver green eyes were full of happy tears.

Mark had found all kinds of miniature items from his store. He had not realized what a booming business miniatures had become. He brought a beautiful huge Victorian dollhouse for the elves and fairies. It sat on a table on the back porch so there could always be interaction. The catalogs he received now were carefully scanned for anything he thought the fairies or elves could use or even enjoy. Some days, after the store was closed, Avery and her dad and stepmom would bring a group of fairies and elves to the store and turn them loose. They loved it.

Dave and Marisa had opened the house to any and all little folk but Dave had one condition. Bathroom visits were private and his and Marisa's bedroom as well. They all laughed but agreed so it was common to see magical people playing about the house, especially the kitchen. They loved helping Marisa cook. Truth be told, she loved it more.

They all made frequent trips to the underground fairy realm and every time they explored, they found something new. It truly was a wondrous place. Both worlds were open for these lucky humans and they knew they were lucky. The little magic people felt that way too because they also had both worlds now.

This may seem like a perfect ending, and it is, for now. Everyone in this extended family knew that they had not seen the last fairy hunter and they had to be especially guarded, but let them be happy now.

Bad Hair Day

———————◆◆◆———————

Young people today are typically equipped with some kind of earbuds. Years ago this kind of listening device was not invented yet, then it was only in the guise of huge headphones with cords that were not long enough to get too far away from the music source. Now you see everyone with very small, white cordless pieces of plastic hanging out of their ears. It might look as though a pigeon hit someone's ear with a fly-by shit torpedo. This practice can start at a very young age but none younger than Beatrice.

As a baby Beatrice watched her parents with these in their ears and thought they were a part of the body. As a toddler, she was already using them but not the little ones. Her nanny got her a pair of actual headphones that could not be swallowed. Her parents both had careers that kept them very busy and the nanny learned the headphones turned out to be a perfect babysitter. Fortunately, Beatrice loved music.

Her parents had never planned to have kids but the first five months of the pregnancy seemed to change them. They were a little excited. She was still able to work and she was having maternal thoughts for once in her life. The last month of her pregnancy changed those feelings though. She no longer had any feelings of motherly love and just wanted that baby out. They would have given the baby up for adoption the second she was born but since they had been showered with gifts from well-wishers and family they only kept her because of guilt. They were fixed financially so they had a full time nanny and like many people, the parents thought that cost was directly indicative to their profession. The more expensive, the better. Since this nanny was expensive they assumed she was good. They were shallow people. Turns out that the nanny was not very maternal either and she knew the parents were not monitoring her at all so she did as little as possible.

Beatrice was a bald baby and did not even get hair until she was almost two years old and then it was just a few little wisps of hair. Just enough to clip a barrette to, proving she was a girl. This was another embarrassment for the parents. By then she was wearing the big headphones and they thought maybe that was a deterrent. Maybe that was rubbing on her head and keeping hair from growing. It did not stop the nanny from using them as a babysitter though and since the parents were not around they said nothing. It was not the headphones though. She had very little hair when she started school. It was almost white and so fine that even the smallest of breezes would blow it around.

Beatrice loved music, it was her only friend. At first, the nanny got her all the music for toddlers but by the time she was five years old she was listening to adult music. The only redeeming factor about the nanny was that she loved the oldies so that is what she provided for Beatrice. When she entered kindergarten the teachers took away her headphones. At first she threw a gigantic tantrum but after she began to interact with the other kids she was happy. This was new to her. She had never played with other children. She had her toys and her music and that was her life. Even at that young age she had no interaction with her parents. The nanny was all she knew. The parents relied on the nanny to see to all her basic needs and provided her with an unlimited credit card to do just that.

By middle school, Beatrice's hair was still almost white, still sparse and wispy. Afraid that the other kids would tease

Beatrice, her nanny bought her a variety of expensive, natural hair wigs, but she would not wear them. She said they muffled her head. She could not even concentrate on her music when she was wearing one because it somehow muffled everything. It was not until Beatrice was in her teens before her hair started to fill out. Almost overnight it went from being practically white, sparse and wispy, to a light strawberry blond. She had never had a haircut. She had never needed one.

The other kids never teased her because they were afraid of her. She was mean. When they played soccer she would intentionally trip or step on other players and sometimes they were on the same team. If someone was in her way she plowed through them. Her teammates loved that about her and hated that about her. If she was on the playing field they rarely lost. She was lightly reprimanded on numerous occasions for pulling another player's hair. Once, during a particularly rough scrimmage she was holding a fistful of hair when it was over. The teachers would tell the other girls to be patient with her because she was not blessed with a full head of hair like they were but also try to keep their distance. The teachers also did not want to lose any of the donations from her parents. Her parents knew that being generous benefactors would go a long way in protecting their daughter. They were not aware that Beatrice was mean and snobby to the other students, but they did not care to hear about her antics at school. That was why they paid the nanny.

It was about this time that Beatrice started hearing the voices. She realized this was what she had been hearing all along but now she could actually make out the words. She thought back to when she was a toddler and she remembered hearing them way back then but she was always plugged into her music so it drowned them out. She wondered if it happened to everyone, these voices but she did not think anyone other than herself could hear them. They had to be in her head. She thought maybe because she was always plugged into some kind of music the voices had to speak louder to be heard above the noise, and that is why she was hearing them now. It was something she needed to talk to someone about but when she brought it up her nanny gave her a crazy look so she dropped it.

Beatrice's hair was growing so fast now it was uncanny. Unfortunately, the voices were getting bolder and louder too but she was the only one that could hear them. The voices went on practically non-stop and sometimes they argued amongst themselves.

As Beatrice was getting ready for school the voices started early.

From a higher voice *"Hey little girl, no ponytail today okay?"*

A little deeper voice *"What's wrong with a pony tail?*

"Oh yeah, of course it's okay with you, you're up there in the middle but for those of us out on the edges we lose six to ten guys for every shittin' ponytail!"

Then the voices all started at once.

"Hey Rapunzel, lay off the curling iron!"

"And the flat iron too! That shit hurts like a mother!"

"Put that son of a bitch against your own belly and see what it feels like!"

"That curling iron too! Why don't you turn that up to hot and jam it up your ass!"

"Don't brush us so hard, we lose a lot of guys that way, you bitch!"

"We can all hear these poor guys crying when you're dumping them in the trash. How can you just throw us away like that?"

"Lay off the hairspray, princess. Can't breathe with that stuff!"

"You're too rough with the damn hairdryer, not so hot!"

"Get a different shampoo! That one tastes like shit!"

"And don't scrub so hard! We have maybe thirty casualties every time you shampoo!"

"And we can hear you scoff at them while they are writhing in pain in the drain!"

"Sleep on the other side once in a while, you're killin' us with your fat head!"

"And get rid of that rap shit you started listening to on your headphones."

"Yeah, next time I hear some of that crap we are all going to start screaming!"

"Go back to the classic rock and roll or you'll be sorry!"

"SHUT UP! SHUT UP! SHUT UP! SHUT UUUUUUUPPPP!" Beatrice yelled.

The nanny rushed to her room to see why she was yelling. She asked, "What the hell is going on? What's wrong? Who are you yelling at?"

"MY HAIR!" yelled Beatrice.

"Your hair? Your hair is talking to you?" asked the nanny.

"My hair is yelling at me. They are all against me. Can't you hear that?" asked Beatrice.

The nanny was very quiet and leaned her head close to Beatrice's.

Her hair was still talking and one group was saying, *"Oooooh, get her away quick. Her dirty hair is about to touch us! Move your head away you moron!"*

Another group of hair joined in and got loud about it. All the sudden the nanny's eyes got wide and she looked at Beatrice and said, "I think I might have heard something."

Beatrice looked relieved when she said, "You did hear something! You really did hear something! Thank God you heard it. I live with this every day, all day. That's why I have my headphones on all the time. Thank God you believe me."

The nanny looked puzzled and said, "Well, I think I heard something but I don't know what it was."

Beatrice grabbed the nanny by the arm and shouted, "You need to go get me some wigs but not natural hair, they have to be synthetic! I'm getting rid of this shit on my head. I can't stand it anymore! Go now!"

The nanny ran out of the room, grabbed her keys, and took off.

The nanny came back with four new wigs. They were all synthetic and the color was close to Beatrice's hair color. The assortment ranged from short to long. She went to Beatrice's room and walked in to see a razor in Beatrice's hand and her completely bald, shiny head. She could tell Beatrice had been crying and when she first spoke, her voice was cracking and cutting in and out so she knew she had been yelling at the top of her lungs also. Beatrice looked at the nanny and said, "I showed them! I showed them all! They're gone now and I hope they hurt! I hope I hurt them all real bad!" Then she looks at the floor and starts stomping on all the hair and yelling, "I hope this hurts, and I hope it hurt when I was cutting you all up! You're all dead now so leave me alone!"

Beatrice was happy with the new wigs. She went to school the next day and for the first time in years she had no headache, and no voices, her head was peaceful. In fact, she felt so good that she was almost nice to the other students. She struck up conversations with them and actually listened. She could picture herself with friends now. She felt good. She was happier than she had been in years. It was the best week. Her nanny noticed the change in her. She was a new person. A nice person.

On Friday, the nanny picked up a smiling and friendly Beatrice from school. They talked and laughed on the way home. Beatrice went to her room and removed her wig. She looked at herself in the mirror and heard nothing. She had hopes for a happier future until she ran her hand across her head and felt all the stubbles. When she did that all the sudden a cacophony of tiny, very high voices began talking all at once.

She heard:

"Hey not so rough with the hands girly! We're new here!"

"Ooooh it's so bright!"
"I feel fantastic!"
"So alive and fresh!"
"Hey there princess, where have you been?"
"Wow everything is so bright and new!"
"I feel loose and young!"
"Yeah, no pain or pressure!"
"And none of that infernal racket she calls music!"
"I feel great too!"
"Hey, we're starting all over again!"
"We are brand new!"
"I think there's more of us now though!"
"Oh yeah, we're coming in heavy now!"
"How long before the princess destroys us now?"
"It doesn't matter, we just feel better and stronger."
"Ooooh, it feels so good to stretch!"

That was all she could stand. "NO, NO, NO, NO, NO!" screamed Beatrice as she reached for the razor.

BARBARA JEAN

◄────────────◆◆◆────────────►

Chapter 1

If someone had told the school counselor, Ms. Lockhart, that there were ghosts she would not have believed them. She would never have called that person a liar though, never. She would have listened intently, even thrown in an 'I see,' or maybe a 'go on' in the appropriate places but would remain a skeptic. She remembered the precise time she became a believer though and that was on October 31st, 1988, the day she died.

Barbara Lockhart had always wanted to be a counselor. After four years of college she went on to earn her masters degree in counseling psychology in record time. She considered going for a PhD but was too excited about going to work and thought that might be something to pursue in a few years, but she never did. She did not want to hang out a shingle, instead she had her heart set on working at her old high school, Central. Central High was a very old school with a large, diverse student body. She had the good fortune of becoming part of the staff there in 1971. She was twenty-three years old.

On the afternoon of October 31st, 1988, a man came into the school and started shooting. Barbara never thought about being a hero but became one that day. She pushed some students into a room, while she confronted the shooter. So far there were no casualties and the man seemed to calm down when Barbara talked. He had lowered his weapon and Barbara was starting to approach him when the police burst into the hall. The shooter was so startled that he lifted his gun and accidentally fired, hitting Barbara. The bullet went right to her heart and she lived only long enough to exchange a sorrowful look with the shooter as the police were putting him in handcuffs. It was her fortieth birthday. Happy fricking birthday Barbara.

The next thing that Barbara remembered was standing in the hallway where she had previously been pronounced dead. She did not know she was dead until one of the other staff members walked by her and did not acknowledge her greeting. In fact, he would have walked right into Barbara if she had not moved. The bell rang, doors were slung open, and students started to pile into the hallway. Barbara tried to get out of the way, but one student was running in her direction. She was trapped, could not move out of the way fast enough so she just closed her eyes and waited for impact. Instead of impact though something utterly weird and extremely ugly happened. Her skin felt like it was being stretched off her body and at the same time her stomach was being pulled up to her mouth. She was so nauseous she knew she was going to hurl and then the feeling was gone. All of it. Even though that awful feeling was rather fleeting she was certain that the anticipated impact would have been much less painful.

The halls had cleared as she recovered from that encounter when she heard a voice from a few feet away. A woman dressed in a seventies style, fringed, summer dress was standing across the hall. She was shaking her head as she said, "You're new, aren't you?"

Barbara looked at her pleadingly and said, "What's happening here? What's going on? New? What do you mean, new?"

Summer dress girl answered, "First of all, Hi, my name is Daisy. Sorry if I frightened you, I know you are very confused and scared."

"Yes, I am," cried Barbara.

Daisy walked over and hugged her, and Barbara hugged back fiercely, and the tears really flowed then.

"Let's go sit down and talk," volunteers Daisy. Barbara nods her head and follows.

Barbara told Daisy all that she remembered, which was not much, but that it felt to her that the shooting just happened. She said, "I remember I was talking to the man with the gun and he was listening to me when all the sudden hell broke loose. Police burst in and scared the shit out of the man, and me, for that matter. He unintentionally jerked the gun up and it fired somewhere in my direction, but he was not purposely shooting at me. It was a nervous reaction. I could see in his eyes that he was at first shocked that he shot, and then sorry. Then everything just disappeared. I don't remember everything going completely black or completely white. I just remember everything was gone and then I was standing in the hall again. I thought maybe I had just had a bad headache and hallucinated some kind of vision until the bell rang, and nobody saw me."

Daisy waited for her to finish and to maybe spill a few more tears before she spoke. "This didn't happen just now. It's been a couple weeks since the shooting. You've been here, kind of, but not fully until just now. I've been waiting and watching you. I wanted to be able to help you when you, well, came to, I guess."

"I don't know what's happening to me," sobbed Barbara. "I'm sorry, my name is Barbara, call me Barb, and you said you are Daisy, right? Daisy, I don't mean to be blunt but what the hell is going on? Why am I seemingly invisible and what on earth happened to me in the hall? And I've worked here for seventeen years and I know all the students, the staff, and the faculty, so why have I never met you before? And lastly, what the hell do you mean about me being here for a couple weeks?"

"Wow," answered Daisy. "Okay, I will try to make this

as painless as possible but I am going to tell you the situation quickly with no sugar coating so please listen carefully, then I will answer all your questions. Okay?"

"Okay," sobbed Barb.

Daisy proceeded to tell Barb all the details since her death. It took a lot of examples to convince Barb that she was in fact, dead. She kept trying to get people in the hall to notice her until finally, she was convinced that they could not see her. Daisy kept warning her as Barb was trying to intercept someone walking down the hall. "Be careful, they'll walk right through you," Daisy told her, "And you already know that's not pleasant."

"Where have I been for the past two weeks after the.... you know, the shooting?" asked Barb.

"Well," Daisy said thoughtfully, "that's not real clear. You were here, but you were not really all here yet. I mean, I could see a little haze and I knew someone was coming. Then you started to take form, at first you were invisible but then you started becoming more visible every day until 'voila' and you're totally here. I know it's weird because all the while you were becoming visible here, you were invisible to them."

"So, I'm a ghost?" asked Barb.

"Yeah, we like the word spirit better, but yep, you're a ghost," answered Daisy. "It's not so bad, once you get used to it. Don't worry, I'll stick with you and teach you the ropes, if you like. I had someone help me when I first went 'spirit', and I don't think I woulda made it without her."

"Yes, I'd like that," said Barb, "I'd like that very much. I love your accent by the way, it reminds me of that lady on the sitcom about a couple in Queens."

Daisy laughed and said, "Thank you. Just like music, huh? Some people don't appreciate the way I talk." She pronounced the word talk more like 'tawk' and she dropped the 'r' at the end of any words ending in 'r.' The difference between her accent and Barb's deep southern accent were like night and day but somehow, they seem to blend nicely.

Daisy told Barb more about being a spirit. They were not anchored to any particular place, in fact, Daisy had only been at the high school for a few weeks. She told her she was actually getting ready to move on when she saw Barb begin to appear, so she decided to stick around to help since nobody else seemed to take notice. Daisy knew that the most pressing questions that Barb would have would be questions Daisy would be unable to answer. Questions like, what are they doing there? Is this heaven? Is it some sort of purgatory? And yes, those were the first questions.

"If this isn't heaven, or hell, or even purgatory," asked Barb, "then have you ever witnessed anyone disappearing suddenly? I mean, like maybe they went into the light? It was their 'AHA' moment when they crossed over, or whatever the hell happens?"

"Like I said before," Daisy answered, "I don't think anyone is actually anchored to their death place so sometimes people just move on and disappear that way. But have I ever seen anyone being struck like they usually show in the movies and the great light appears and then they disappear, no. Again, I have only been here for a few weeks, so I have only met a few people. I have moved around a lot, I've stayed in this area but I move around a lot. I get restless I guess, and depressed. I've met a lot of people but you're the first one I have stuck around to help."

Barb looked at Daisy and said, "I don't understand why I would end up here and not in heaven, if there even is a heaven. I think my biggest sin was stealing a pack of gum when I was seven years old! Nope, this is not what anyone would expect from God. He must be gone, if he ever was here. This is just plain screwed up."

Daisy could see Barb was losing it so she went to her, put her arms around her and said, "Barb, I think everyone here, or at least those of us who could even put a thought together in their head, has felt the same."

Barb started sobbing and Daisy could barely make out her next words, "fuck this."

Daisy nodded and held Barb. She agreed and said, "Yeah this is some kind of fucked up."

Daisy and Barb talked solid for the next two days. Daisy told Barb all about navigating the spirit world and Barb told Daisy what she had missed since 1974. Daisy was amazed at how uptight and seemingly self-righteous the world was becoming. She had witnessed some of the major changes, but Barb was able to tell her more because she lived it. After only a couple of days together, they each considered the other to be a wealth of information and were happy to have found each other. Barb could not thank Daisy enough for waiting and helping her.

After they had covered some of the past living that Daisy missed, and the future ghost living for her, Barb started to tell Daisy about some of her acquaintances at school. She pointed out the bullies, the jocks, the cheerleaders, the nerds, the problem students, and the shy ones. She introduced Daisy, the introductions being only one-sided, of course, to some of the staff and faculty. She got to know many of these students on a more personal level, as their counselor, some of the faculty as well.

There was one student in particular, Joe, of which she had grown very fond. Barb had gotten to know him through counseling. He was smart and attractive but because he was painfully shy, he was never considered a popular kid. Another kid with the same MO was Elly. Both kids were smart and attractive and attracted to each other. Barb was the only one who knew this because she had counseled both and they opened up to her about their feelings. She was fond of them and wanted to help.

When Barb told Daisy, "I think I could help Joe with minimal encouragement if I could somehow get closer to him," Daisy reminded Barb about the pain she endured when someone walked through her.

Daisy shot back, "And what makes you think you have any control from the inside? I have been spirit living a long time and I've never heard of anyone doing that on purpose."

"I don't know," said Barb, "but I just feel like I have to try. He's such a good kid, and I'm just scared he will get lost in the shuffle if he never comes out of his shell a little. And I would never encourage him to say anything to Elly if I knew she didn't like him too. She has the same problem, only not as severe. It's a little easier for girls though. Anyway, I truly believe that if they got together, it would boost confidence in them both. They are both seniors now and I can't stand the thought of them both spending the rest of this year like they are now. So, are you going to help me?"

Daisy smiled as she said, "You are not going to let this go, are you?"

Barb smiled back, "Nope."

Daisy said, "I don't even know if you can do what you are trying to do, and I sure don't know how. Like I told you before, I don't know of anybody who has jumped into a 'live one' on purpose."

"Well, I'm going to be your first then," said Barb, "What else do we have to do in this spirit world unless we participate? Just watch? No, not me."

Daisy's eyes got wide as she said, "Ooh, I believe I like you Ms. Barbara Jean Lockhart! You are the most exciting person I have known in years!"

They both laughed and Barb said, "Let's find a time when Joe is alone, and we can try our experiment."

Chapter 2

A guidance counselor's focus in on vocational guidance but Barb was a school counselor, meaning she helped students, and faculty and their families, not only with their academics but with career, social, and emotional development. Because Barb's field of counseling encompassed more, she was able to thoroughly know the students, and faculty, at both educational and personal levels.

Barb and Daisy knew it might not be easy to find a time when Joe was alone for any measurable amount of time, but the opportunity presented itself just a day later. Joe's class before lunch had been cancelled so he walked outside, sat under a tree, and pulled out a book.

Barb looked at Daisy and said, "I'm goin' in." She was not sure how to do this so she walked over to Joe, sat down in the same position, then slid over with her shoulder next to his. She pushed into him a little but it was very painful. She kept trying to do it slowly and it was hurting more every time. She tried a little more force but that pain was horrible and it forced her out after only about an inch. She was getting frustrated and the pain was so great that she was holding her breath after that last jolt. Still holding her breath she slipped into Joe easily and painlessly. "Shit Daisy, I'm in!"

Barb had slipped into Joe. "Good Lord, Daisy, you should hear this. I forgot what it was like to be a teenager. I'm hearing this in his head *'wonder what that test will / she was wearing a / oh no forgot to clean the / what is that sound / Is that a mosquito / shit Daisy I'm in / who's Daisy and I'm in what? / there's Elly so pretty / good lord daisy you should hear this / hear what? / why didn't she smile? / wow that sun is really / did I wash my hands? / Elly's going to walk by / oh look at that squirrel....'* uh oh." Barb wondered how she was going to get his attention when right at that moment Elly was walking down the path directly in front of him.

Barb thought to herself 'I've got to get him up somehow, now, so she said out loud GET UP JOE, GET UP, GET UP' and Joe started to get up. If she could get him walking now, he would meet Elly. He started walking. Barb was ecstatic. She yelled to him SAY HELLO TO ELLY! SAY HELLO TO ELLY! and he did. Barb was hoping that just by getting Joe to break the ice with Elly that she might take over and start a conversation, and she was right. Elly looked up at Joe with the biggest smile ever, said hello, then asked him something about one of the classes, and the conversation began.

Barb jumped out of Joe.

"Well, don't you look like the cat that ate the canary!" laughed Daisy.

Barb had a very satisfied look on her face as she laughed along with Daisy. "Okay, here's the deal. First of all, if you hold your breath, you can slip right in, no pain. I kinda found that out the hard way but I know now! Also, I tried talking to you and he heard that, sort of. It was jumbled in with all the other thoughts on his mind but it was there so I couldn't tell you what I was doing. He was briefly confused about why he was thinking about a daisy that should hear something. I tell ya, I had totally forgotten what went on inside a teenager's head. It's a busy place."

"So it didn't hurt?" asked Daisy.

"It hurt like the dickens at first," answered Barb, "all those times I was trying to get inside until the last one it hurt so bad I had to hold my breath, that's when I discovered you can jump in if you hold your breath. It's not at all like when they run through you, so now I wonder if you held your breath when they did maybe it wouldn't hurt."

Daisy added, "Well, it's for sure that Joe didn't feel a thing. He didn't even flinch when you went in or came out."

They both stood and watched as Joe and Elly walked down the path together. Barb broke the silence, "You have got to do that Daisy! It's almost like you are alive again, I mean not really, but you can feel the body move like it's yours. Can you imagine what this means?"

"No," said Daisy, "but I'm listening."

"You've been a spirit now for a long time, right," as Daisy nodded Barb continued, "well, like I said, it felt like I was standing up, I felt the body like it was mine. The head not so much, but we can work on that. So, Daisy, how long has it been since you rode a bike? Or went horseback riding? Or had your first kiss? Can't you see, we can experience all those things again, by proxy, now that we know how to jump into a person. It doesn't hurt the person, in fact, what I did with Joe was wonderful, but we could be undetected if we just wanted to experience what they are doing at the time. We could go to the airport and piggyback someone who is skydiving, if that's your cup of tea. One thing, we wouldn't have to worry about falling to our death but if we decided we didn't want to continue all we would have to do is hold our breath and leave the person. See what I'm saying? Our little world just got a lot bigger!"

"Oh my God!" cried Daisy, "You have discovered something amazing, unless maybe that doesn't work for me."

"Well, we can find that out right now," Barb said, "if you want to."

Daisy looked at Barb with a little uncertainty but said, "I'm scared, but I do want to try. Will you help me?"

Barb smiled and said, "Of course."

There were plenty of people milling about so Barb looked around and saw a young girl sitting on a bench. She was quietly watching a couple of senior boys showing off on their skateboards. Barb pointed her out to Daisy and said, "That girl right there, go jump inside her. Remember though, you need to be quiet, then come back out."

"Okay, here I go," said Daisy. She sat down beside the girl and slid over to join her but bounced back and yelled, "Shit, oh shit, oh shit, that hurts."

Barb had to remind her again, "Remember you have to hold your breath, both going in and coming out."

"Shit, that hurts like a son of a bitch!" cried Daisy. "I forgot to hold my breath but now I'm scared to try it again." Barb gave her the stink eye, as Daisy would call it, so she said, "Alright, alright, I'll try again." This time she took a deep breath and slid inside easily. After about a minute she was back out with a big smile on her face. She said, "Wow, you were right about how busy it is in there. I honestly couldn't keep up with all the thoughts in her head! But it is amazing!"

"It's almost like being in our own body! I felt it when she scratched an itch and when she crossed her legs and when she suppressed a burp, it was amazing! I can't wait to do it again and I know just who I'm jumping into this time!"

"We have to be careful though," said Barb, "we should really keep this to ourselves. If the other spirits know we can do this, it could cause havoc." Daisy looked at her with questioning eyes as Barb added, "Don't you see? If all the spirits learn, and they are all able to do this, they would jump in someone and change that poor person into their own. We can't take over people's lives like that."

"You're right," said Daisy, "but you and I can still have fun though, right? I mean we can still just jump into someone to experience the thrill of something again, right? They don't even have to know that we are there."

"Yes," answered Barb, "but we still can't tell anyone else. Promise me you won't say anything to anyone else. And we can't piggyback anyone when other spirits are around or they will see us. I mean it too."

"Yes," said Daisy, "I promise I will never tell. But there's lot of stuff I want to experience again and one of them is going on right now. Those skateboard boys are behind that building smoking a joint and I want to experience that again, right now. Come on!"

They both joined the skateboarders behind the shed right then but they vowed they would never reveal their secret to another spirit. They did not say a word while they were experiencing the joint, they may have giggled a little, but the boys did not notice.

Barb knew a lot of the students and all the faculty. She knew that most of the students were good kids, but some just needed a little encouragement, or maybe discouragement, so she still 'helped' them a little from the inside. She felt she was qualified to give a little nudge in the right direction when it was needed but that was all she ever did. A couple of weeks had passed since she 'nudged' Joe to talk to Elly and now they were holding hands. Their lives had improved in all areas since they both achieved more confidence.

Chapter 3

Daisy and Barb quickly became best friends and experienced many things that they thought would never happen again. They had become pretty close with the smoking skateboard seniors too and thought it was fortunate that the seniors had welcomed some lower classmen to join. Now Barb and Daisy could continue to enjoy this after the seniors had graduated.

They exchanged stories about their past lives. How they lived, how they died. Daisy died in a car accident in 1974. Her boyfriend and her were at a stoplight when a car hit them from behind. The car was ten years old and not equipped with seatbelts. Daisy went through the windshield. She was twenty-three years old.

When she was able to move around as a spirit, she looked for her boyfriend. He had been released from the hospital so she went to his house only to find that he had moved. She was happy that he had lived but she missed him. It was a very bittersweet time for her. For some strange reason she was still drawn to visit her accident site. Maybe she thought he would visit when he became a spirit and they would reconnect.

Barb met her fiancé in college. He went on to medical school. During his last year they became engaged. Two weeks before the wedding he was in a fatal car accident. Barb never fell in love again. She was twenty-six years old.

Daisy took Barb to the accident site where she died. She visited it often but she did not know why. Maybe she thought if her boyfriend died he would come looking for her and this was the last place they were together. It was always sad. Daisy joined Barb as she visited the site where her fiance had been killed. Maybe her thoughts were similar to Daisy. Maybe she thought he may show up there again some day. The ladies did this every week or two and then had a good cry together.

Over the next few weeks, the girls enjoyed things they

thought would never happen again and things they would never have tried while they lived. Driving a motorcycle and even riding a skateboard was big for them both, but so far, one of the best, was experiencing the first kiss. The pure unadulterated exhilaration of that was beyond compare. Daisy never talked or interfered in any way with her host. She just went along for the ride. She would sometimes alert Barb of someone that may need a little guidance. Daisy knew she was not qualified to do that and she really did not know how Barb did it anyway. It worked out very well.

The first instance where Daisy had to get Barb's help was when her 'ride-along' was trying skateboard tricks that he knew he could be hurt and it did not phase him. In fact, he looked forward to it. Daisy did not think it was exactly suicidal but it was definitely too dangerous for him to be attempting especially when he was wanting to fail. Barb piggy-backed during one of these excursions and put mental pictures in his head of him hurt, or worse, and what it would do to his family. She showed him how this was selfish on his part and she talked about family. He was basically a good kid, a little mixed up but good, and her counseling seemed to work on him.

Barb had helped Joe and Elly find each other and in doing that, it helped with their shyness and little by little they were shedding their shells. They developed relationships with other students and were happy. The only other problem that Joe had was with tests. He was terrified of them and so he did not do well even though he knew the answers. Barb was determined to help him in this area.

It was test day for Joe. This was a big one that stood for half of the final grade. He would probably still pass history if he did not get a good grade on it but it would be a barely passing grade. Barb had to help. She slid into Joe in time to experience the absolute fear he felt as the tests were handed out. The feeling was so intense Barb was tempted to jump right out but she knew she had to help. Joe picked up his pencil and looked at the test. Barb whispered, "It's okay Joe.

No need to fear this test." Barb could feel what she thought might be just the least bit of ease so she continued, "You know this Joe, you've got this." Joe started answering the questions. His tension lessened. "Joe, you know this stuff." Joe cocked his head like he was trying to remember something and then blurted out loud, "Miss Lockhart!"

The history teacher at the front of the classroom looked at Joe and said, "Yes Joe, we all miss her, Miss Lockhart was a great counselor."

Joe said, "No, she's in my" he started to say head but he just stopped. Everyone was still looking at him and just so they would not think he was insane, he more calmly said, "I mean she's just on my mind, I miss her." He knew Miss Lockhart though. He knew how she could always calm him. He thought to himself it would be great if she really were still in touch with him because he missed her. He thought, 'I wish you were with me Miss Lockhart.'

She answered, "I am." She could not help herself. He wanted her there. "Please stay calm, lets finish this test. You don't need to talk out loud, I hear your thoughts. Afterward, we can talk a little."

With his fear of tests severely calmed by Barb, Joe finished and felt good about it. He walked outside and sat down under a tree. He said, "Miss Lockhart, is that really you?"

He got a funny look from someone walking by as Barb said, "Yes, Joe, it's me, and remember you don't have to talk out loud, I can hear your thoughts. People will think you're crazy."

Joe lowered his head and thought, 'I just miss you so much. You were the only one I could talk to. You were the only one that understood me and actually wanted to help me.'

"Joe, I know that's not true," said Barb. "It's just that you didn't know where to look. You've told me about your parents, and I've met your mom. She loves you very much and you can talk to her, she's just waiting for you to open up to her. And I've missed you too but just to let you know, I don't know how much longer I can 'haunt' you, or even if I can ever do this again."

Joe thought, *'You've been with me before today, haven't you? You helped me with Elly, didn't you? I was too shy to even say hello and all the sudden I walked over to her. That was you helping me wasn't it?'*

"Yes. But that was all you needed. Just a little nudge," said Barb. "Just like taking tests. You know the material, you just don't like the test. Maybe now you see that can be okay too."

'But you don't have to leave me now, do you?' thought Joe.

"Well, I think you are fine without me now," answered Barb, "don't you?"

Joe's thought was almost out before Barb finished, *'No,'* he thought. *'It's like I only feel confident when you are near.'*

"But if I had not answered you," said Barb, "then you would never have known I was with you. I'm afraid I may have made a big mistake."

'No, that's not true.' thought Joe. *'I knew something, or someone, was somehow helping me. I could feel it. It was surreal, and great. It was the confidence I never had. Ms. Lockhart I miss you. Don't leave me now.'*

"I'm not going to leave you right now Joe," said Barb. "But soon. And since we are so close now, maybe you should call me Barb. I have to tell you though that I'm not in here all the time. I just slipped in for your test and I was going to jump right back out after I saw that you just needed that little nudge again. I can't believe you recognized me. But remember, I have met your parents, and you have a great support system there. Let them help you. Open up to them. Your mom can help you as much as I can, you just have to let her."

'I will, I promise, Barb, but please,' pleaded Joe's thought, *'don't leave me now.'*

"I'm going to leave now but I'll revisit you, I promise that." said Barb. "I have made a friend here in the spirit world and I still have lots to learn about where I am but I'm not leaving this area anytime soon, so you might be sick of me. I won't be piggy-backing you every day but I promise I will be here for a while."

Barb slid out of Joe and found Daisy immediately. In the spirit world, one did not really have to walk or run or have any mode of transportation to relocate. Barb discovered that she just needed to think about a place and she was there.

Chapter 4

After eight months of being a school spirit, Barb found the moment very bittersweet when she thought about Joe and Elly. They were going to graduate and they were both becoming very popular. She was going to miss them but she had also thought about possibly moving for a while. Graduation was in two weeks, then summer vacation when most everyone would be gone. A few might have summer school but this might be a chance for her to go somewhere else for a while. She would have to talk to Daisy about it.

Barb found Daisy and asked, "Daisy, what are we going to do during summer vacation? Everyone will be gone, it will be too lonely here."

"I've not been here during summer vacation," said Daisy. "I had just been here a couple weeks before I saw you so I hung around."

"Where were you before?" asked Barb.

"Well, this might sound silly to you, but for some reason I just want to stick around close to where I died. I know there's probably no sense in doing that because my boyfriend is now thirty-seven years old, he and I were both twenty-three when I died. Then she looked at Barb and said, "Isn't it kind of funny how you were born in 1948 and I was born in 1951 so there should be only three years age difference between us, but since you lived longer than me there's really about seventeen years difference. That's crazy."

"Are you calling me old?" snickered Barb.

They both laughed and Daisy said, "I feel like we are both the same age. You are the best friend I've ever had."

"I feel the exact same way!" said Barb.

Joe asked Barb if she would be with him during Graduation. He was so grateful for everything she had done for him that he felt she should share his big day. This touched Barb deeply and she told him she would be honored, so Barb was front and center on his big day. She stuck around long enough to see that his relationship with his parents had progressed immensely. She was so proud of the young man that he was becoming and so pleased to hear him credit her for the new him. It was sad when Barb said goodbye but Joe refused to call this the end of the relationship. Obviously, they could not exchange telephone numbers but Joe told her his college plans and made her promise that she would visit him.

The next day the girls went to Daisy's accident site. Daisy said, "I'm kind of glad we're spirits, this neighborhood is getting kind of sketchy."

"Well, there's a positive spin on our condition," laughed Barb.

As if on cue a young man ran to an old dented Chevrolet and jumped in. He was trying to get it started and the engine was not turning over. The car just growled as he cussed and hit the steering wheel. Sirens could be heard in the near distance but getting closer. Daisy told Barb, "I've seen that guy before, I think he lives around here. I think maybe he is a dealer but I've only seen him with marijuana."

Just then another man runs up and gets in the car. He pulls out a knife, stabs the driver, drops a gun in his lap, gets out of the car and runs away. The sirens are within a couple blocks now, getting closer.

"Oh no," cried Daisy "that guy stabbed him and left him

for the cops. He planted that gun on him too. I bet he shot someone with that and is planting the blame on him."

Two police cars pulled up and surrounded the Chevrolet with the stabbed man inside. Daisy started walking closer to the car. Barb said, "No Daisy, where are you going? You can't do anything."

The Chevrolet door opened and the driver stepped out. The blood was still spreading from his stab wound. He was holding the gun but his arms were up. The policemen were aiming their guns at him and yelling for him to drop the gun. Daisy could see that he was hurt and confused so she ran to him.

"Daisy, what are you doing? Stay away from there!" yelled Barb.

"He's hurt and he doesn't know what he's doing Barb! He needs to drop the gun or they will shoot him. I'm going to help him!" cried Daisy.

"Daisy, no!" cried Barb. "Get away from him, come back here!"

The police were still yelling at him to drop the weapon when Daisy slipped inside. She could feel all the hurt and confusion he felt. She started to tell him to drop the gun and he began to lower the arm that held the weapon. She yelled out for Barb, "It's working! He's going to be okay! I did it Barb!" That's when he stopped lowering the arm with the gun and instead pointed it at his own head and fired. His body fell to the ground.

"Daisy!" yelled Barb. "Daisy, where are you?" She was yelling at the top of her lungs. She kept calling her name over and over again but she saw no sign of Daisy. She ran over to the dead body and tried to slip inside but was not able. "Why can't I get inside you? I have to get Daisy! Please, let me get inside you!" She kept trying until she just could not try anymore. She kept calling Daisy's name until the body was picked up and the police were gone. She wanted to go with the body but she could not slip inside so it would be useless. She wondered if Daisy was trapped inside. If she could not slip inside it only made sense that Daisy would not be able to slip outside. "What happened to you Daisy? Where are you?" Barb sat on the curb, crossed her arms on top of her knees, laid her head down on them and cried. When she finally looked up there was nobody at the scene. She had been there all night. She lost her best friend.

Barb finally rose, gave the scene a final look, and called for Daisy once more. She was so sad she had no idea what she was going to do without her. She hung her head again and when she looked up she found herself at her fiance's accident scene. It was just too much for her. She sat on the curb and lowered her head on her crossed arms and started crying again. She was holding nothing back while she sobbed uncontrollably for both Daisy and her fiance now.

Then she heard a familiar voice. "I've been waiting for you."

Barb looked up and through a blur of tears she could see her fiancé standing in a beam of bright light. She said, "What? Is that you Ralph? Is it really you?"

Ralph said, "It's really me and I've been waiting for you."

"But my friend, Daisy, I've lost her. I've missed you so much Ralph," cried Barb.

Ralph walked over to her, held out his hand, and said, "I'm here to take you home with me. We can look for Daisy together."

Barb took his hand, stood up and hugged Ralph for the first time in a long time. It was a very good hug.

BETWEEN WIFE AND DEATH

◆◆◆

Part 1

Paula and Chase liked to think they were on the verge of wealth. They were both young professionals with soon to be high paying careers and aside from Chase's severe peanut allergy, and sleep apnea, they were both in the best of health. Paula enjoyed teasing Chase about these conditions, calling him defective.

Chase was an architect at a big firm headquartered in a large city. It took a while for him to get where he was, and it would have been impossible had it not been for his wife. Paula sacrificed her career, as wives so often do, until Chase was firmly planted in a world renown architectural firm.

After a couple years of college, Paula had to quit and go to work so they could afford to get Chase through a five-year Bachelor of Architecture degree program. She went to work at a small interior decorating business in town. She always had an eye for interior decorating so this was something she enjoyed, but only until she could continue toward her passion of interior design. It was not long before Paula gained a following and could have called this her career forever and that is exactly what Chase urged her to do because he informed her then that he would need more education. Paula reluctantly agreed to continue working until Chase earned his master's degree in architecture.

Paula had worked, waited, and pushed back her dream

for an additional six years for Chase and she was ready for her turn. She had been the maid and the cook, and given Chase's peanut allergy, that was not always easy. So, when Chase approached her with the news that he still needed a year of practical work experience, and an internship to become certified and licensed, Paula politely told him to go screw himself. She told him she had sacrificed six years for his career and was finished. She was going to go back to school immediately and his job, his practical experience as he called it, would have to be their only income now until she had finally pursued her dream. He was not happy, but he knew he had lost that battle.

Paula finished college with a four-year interior design degree, but she was not finished yet. Chase tried to object but his objections fell on deaf ears. She would need an additional two years of architectural studies and experience to pass the three-part NCIDQ (National Council for Interior Design Qualification) exam and she intended to do just that. After all, she was just asking for four years of his support when she had given him a full six years.

After Paula passed her NCIDQ exam she was ready to join the design world. Chase suggested she join his company, but she did not think they should be working that close in proximity every day, so she secured a position at a different, smaller, architectural firm in town.

Chase was now secure in his position and Paula was happy in hers. Now they were the young professionals on their way to the high-level lifestyles of which they had dreamed.

Chase and Paula had a rather eclectic circle of friends. There was a couple from their old neighborhood, and a couple from college, these were the 'poor' ones in the bunch. Most of the newer friends were from Chase's architect firm. Since most of these people had been there before Chase started, Paula and Chase could be considered the 'poor' couple to them. One exception was Melba. Melba was an interior designer who worked with the architects at Chase's firm. She and Paula quickly became fast friends and not only because they were both designers but because they seemed to have a lot in common. Maybe a little too much.

The firm where Chase and Melba worked had corporate meetings every other Friday. Since it was about a five hour drive, Chase usually drove to the city on Thursday afternoon, spent the night, then drove home after the meeting on Friday. Paula and Melba spent those Thursday nights to hang out together. They would go to the movies, or go bowling, or sometimes to the local nightclub. Regardless, they were always together, until the new convention center was slated to be built in town. Chase's firm was hired, and Melba was needed for all the planning as well. That is when Melba started going on the bi-weekly corporate trips with Chase.

Part 2

Paula had always missed Chase when he had gone to his meetings but now, she was alone. Before, she always had Melba and they were constantly doing things while Chase was away, now she was more lonely than ever. The first couple of weeks were not too bad, Paula went to the movies alone, not as much fun, but it passed a little time. Around the third trip though, Paula was feeling lonelier than ever. Of course, she missed Chase, but she had to admit that she missed Melba even more. She missed their girl's night out. That week she went to bed very sad. When she could not fall asleep right away, she reached over and grabbed Chase's pillow, laid her head on it, and fell asleep.

The next morning Paula woke with a start and sat straight up in bed. She could not remember right away why she awoke like that but later in the morning it hit her. She had a real disturbing dream. She had dreamt that there was something going on between Chase and another woman. She sat at the kitchen table and willed herself into remembering all she could about this unsettling dream. She knew it was ridiculous, of course, but she wanted to recall all that she could about it. Was it an affair? Chase was in a hotel bedroom with another woman. The other woman though was blurred out in her dream. Like when they blur out stuff on TV. There was not one thing about this woman that she could recognize. It was odd, and it was disturbing, but she told herself it was also just a dream and tried to put it out of her mind.

A month later, Paula grabbed Chase's pillow again, and again she woke with a start. That dream returned. The woman in the dream was so well camouflaged that she could not tell if she was dark or light, tall or short, thin or heavy, all she knew was that it was a woman, and she was in the room with Chase. She punched Chase's pillow and said, "Why are you doing this to me?"

That week she decided to do something that she could never talk Chase into doing with her, she signed up for a dance class that met every other Thursday night.

The class was taught by an award-winning brother and sister team, Max and Marnie, with television exposure in their past. Most of the students were couples, and the few singles that participated had already paired up since Paula had missed the first class. She could see that she was the odd person out so as she turned to walk toward the exit she was gently grabbed and pulled into a dance position by the brother of the dancing team, Max. They stood face to face when Max asked, "You aren't walking out on us now, are you?"

Paula looked at him and stuttered, "Well, I can see there are only pairs here and I don't want to make anyone share their time so I will just wait and maybe take a class when I can start from the beginning."

"No, no, not on your life," said Max. "You haven't missed much and I would love to be your partner. I can show you in just a few minutes what we covered in the first class and I would bet that you are a quick learner. In fact you already look like a dancer. So, will you stay?"

"Only if you insist that I'm not putting you out in any way," answered Paula.

"It's settled then, I am your partner. While Marnie is reviewing with the rest of the class," said Max, "We will go over here and I will catch you up with the steps. Don't worry, they are simple. Okay?"

Paula nodded and they went off to the side where Max showed her what the class did in the first session. She learned in record time, and they were able to join the rest of the students after about twenty minutes.

Paula loved the class. It turned out that maybe what Max had said about her looking like a dancer may have been true. She picked up the steps in no time and had fun doing it. Maybe it was because she was paired with one of the instructors, but she felt as if she was ahead of the other students, and this was her first class. She absolutely loved it, and since he was very easy on the eyes, Max was certainly a perk.

Part 3

After a little over two months of dance class Paula noticed the changes in her body and her mind. She was in better shape physically and mentally. It showed at work too. She was doing so well at work that she was given a promotion. Her body was morphing into a more muscular, lithe body than she ever had, even in college. She was happy.

That very night, after dance class, Paula joined the others for a couple drinks after class. This was a little tradition with the class and Paula had bowed out before, but she was glad that she joined this time. It was so much fun that she hated to leave. Max was a big flirt, but she knew he did that all the time, and with everyone. It was still flattering. The rest of the class always commented on the great chemistry that Paula and Max had dancing. Paula felt the chemistry as well, but she also felt chemistry with Chase. That night, maybe feeling a little guilty about her feelings, Paula grabbed Chase's pillow and fell asleep on it.

The next morning Paula bolted awake and sat straight up in bed. She felt a strong sense of Déjà vu. As she got ready for work, she started to remember what she had dreamt. It was another woman again. Chase was having an affair. This time she did not just laugh it off. It felt very real. This feeling was so strong but then again, she did not believe that she and Chase had grown apart. She refused to believe that but why was she having these dreams? There has to be some kind of explanation. She knew these were more than dreams. There had to be some kind of truth in there and she would have to find it.

That weekend they had a dinner party for a few of the people from Chase's office. At one point Melba and Paula were able to sneak off and have a little talk. Paula asked Melba some questions about their trips to the corporate office. Paula noticed that some of the questions appeared to make Melba a little uncomfortable, and that made her even more curious. She asked Melba, "Am I making you uncomfortable? If so, why?"

"No, well, yeah," answered Melba. "Are you checking up on Chase, or on me?"

"Oh, Melba," gushed Paula, "I trust you implicitly! You are my best friend. I can't believe you would even think that! It's about Chase, not you, and I have no reason other than a silly recurring dream. A nightmare really."

Melba's eyebrows shot up as she asked, "What are you talking about? Is he acting differently at home? Maybe a little more distant?" Then in almost a whisper she added, "Maybe you haven't had sex in a while or he's just not that into it when you two, you know?"

"Oh that's not it at all," said Paula. "He's been more into it than ever the last few months! I can't even pass him in the hall without him grabbing me! I'm not complaining, mind you. He's still frisky!"

Melba snickered a little when she asked again, "So you've had a dream and that's what all this is about?"

"Yes, it's a dream," said Paula, "but it's one that I've had at least three times that I can remember. And it's so real. I mean it. Don't laugh at me but I think it's more of a vision. So, I need you to tell me what goes on every other Thursday night because it's driving me crazy."

"Paula, it's not a vision for Christ's sake," snapped Melba. "It's just a dream."

Part 4

Paula glared at Melba and said, "Okay then, tell me what goes on there. I mean everything. I know you guys don't have your meetings until Friday so I guess you go to dinner after you check in at the hotel, right? Who is at the meetings? Do I know everyone there? Who goes out to dinner with you on Thursday nights? Who spends most time with Chase? And especially is he alone after dinner? Do you spend time in his hotel room after dinner?"

"Stop!" Melba almost shouted. "Okay, calm down and I'll try to answer your questions."

Paula was almost in tears when she said, "I'm sorry. I guess it's bothering me more than I thought. The first couple times I had the dream I didn't think anything of it but it's so consistent. It's so frustrating because I can see the woman, but I can't identify her. And this is all only when I lay my head on Chase's pillow!"

Melba's head snapped up when she heard that and she asked, "You can see her? And you have no idea who she is? Better yet, just don't sleep on his pillow anymore!" Melba stared at her after she asked this question. She so much wanted to tell Paula that her vision was right and that she was the woman who spent each night, all night, with Chase. But she could not tell her that. Lord knows she had tried everything to get him to notice her, but he had not taken her up on it, yet. She was sure that Chase was her soulmate, not Paula's. He just did not know it yet. She would try again, one last time, on their next trip but if he again did not reciprocate her feelings, she would do something drastic. She knew that she could not live without him but if he did not feel the same, she would take him away from Paula too.

"What are you thinking about?" asked Paula. "I see you know something that you're not telling me."

Melba looked at Paula and said, "Well, I go to Chase's room after dinner. If it's still early we sometimes play a couple hands of gin rummy. It might be me that you are seeing in your dreams. So, you haven't told Chase about these dreams?"

"No, I haven't said a word to him." said Paula. "I can't tell you how, but I just know that my husband is faithful and believe me, this woman is not wanting to play cards with my husband. She is there for something far more personal than a game of gin rummy. I can feel it. I hate to ask you this, but would you do me a big favor?"

"Sure," answered Melba, "What do you need me to do?"

"On your next trip, would you try to stay a little longer in my husband's room? I mean after dinner you could go back with him and maybe play a few more hands of cards than usual? Pay attention if he gets any phone calls or maybe someone tries to pay him a visit. I'm thinking it has to be someone at corporate who knows he is there. And alone. There is a woman there that has designs on my husband, I just know it."

"Of course," said Melba, "I'll stay as long as he lets me." Melba could not believe it. It was like she was being given the keys to Chase's bedroom by none other than his wife. Oh, she would try to stay with Chase as long as possible, all night if she was lucky. Maybe this time she would even wear him down and she would end up in his bed. She would be a gift to him from his wife. It was like a bad joke but with a happy ending for her.

Part 5

When the next corporate meeting came around Melba had packed her little overnight case with a little more care. A brand new, sexy, negligee laid right on top of her other clothes. She had it all planned in her head. They would go out to dinner, where she would ply Chase with more drinks than normal. When they got to his room, more drinks again.

That Thursday came and Melba started her little fantasy plan in the car on the way to the city. Since it was just her and Chase, she decided to try to steer the conversation to relationships. After all, she was a devious woman with a serious need, Chase. She was not above lying to get what she wanted so she decided to plant some doubt in Chase's head. She knew men were easy to manipulate if you knew how to do it.

Melba knew that Chase would have no reason to question remarks she made about Paula, her best friend. She decided to plant some doubt as she started the conversation with Chase. She asked, "So, what has Paula been doing on these nights that we have to attend the meetings?"

Chase said, "Oh, come on Melba, I know she's told you about her dance classes. We've all talked about it."

"Yeah," said Melba, "I just wondered how you feel about them?"

Chase interrupted her and said, "We're here. You wanna just meet in the restaurant in an hour?"

Melba answered, "Yeah, that's good. We can finish our conversation then."

They met at the restaurant and the hostess greeted them both by name. They were regular customers there. She was still talking to them as they were seated when the waiter walked over. The hostess reminded the waiter that Chase had a nut allergy and to make sure the kitchen knew. The waiter nodded agreement and took their orders.

Over dinner Melba again brought up the subject they

were discussing in the car, Paula's dance class. She looked at Chase and asked him, "So, how do you feel about Paula's dance class, and more importantly about her 'dance' partner?" When she said the word 'dance' she used air quotes.

Chase almost choked on his drink when he said, "What the hell is that supposed to mean? You put the word dance in air quotes. Are you trying to imply something?"

"No, not at all," said Melba. "Just wanting to get how you really feel about them."

"What do you mean, how do I feel about 'em?" answered Chase. "She loves the dance classes and if we ever get to stop these stupid meetings, I'm gonna go with her. They sound like fun and she's getting really good. She shows me what they learn every week. I'm kinda jealous."

"I can see why you should be jealous," smirked Melba.

"What's that supposed to mean? Are you saying I should be jealous of something other than the dancing?" snapped Chase emphasizing the word should.

"Oh, well, you know since she was single when she started classes and she didn't have a partner, one of the instructors volunteered to be hers," snickered Melba, "and from what I understand, he's very hot."

"You mean she told you that?" asked Chase. "Why are you saying this shit? Aren't you supposed to be Paula's best friend? If I didn't know better, I'd think you were trying to stir up some shit, but that can't be right, is it?"

"Oh, come on," Melba spit out a little louder than she should, "you can't tell me that you haven't thought about it. Paula and some hot dude dancing cheek to cheek and belly to belly. You can't be that secure!"

"Keep your voice down, and yes, I'm secure!" Chase tried not to yell. In a quieter voice he said, "Why the hell are you doing this? You're her best friend, aren't you? I think you're making this shit up, but why? What on earth could you possibly gain from talking like this?"

"Chase," Melba said just above a whisper, "You're right.

I'm so sorry. I don't know what got into me. Can I blame it on hormones? Please forgive me. Can we go back to your room and talk a little? Maybe I can explain why I've been acting so shitty."

"Maybe we should just call it a night tonight and see each other in the meeting tomorrow," said Chase.

"No, please," pleaded Melba, "at least let me explain myself."

"Okay," relented Chase.

"I have to run to the ladies room real quick, I'll be right back," said Melba.

She excused herself to visit the restroom as she grabbed an empty pill bottle from her purse and slipped into the kitchen instead. She scanned the room looking for something and when she spied it she was able to fill her pill bottle and again slip out of the kitchen without being seen. Then she met Chase at the elevator and they went up to their rooms. In the elevator Melba slipped her room keycard into Chase's jacket pocket. As the elevator doors opened Chase looked at Melba and said, "I changed my mind, I'm tired and I don't want to talk to you anymore tonight so I'll see you in the morning."

Melba gave him a sad look but said, "But it's only 9:00." When he did not respond she said, "Okay. See you in the morning." They both walked toward their respective rooms. Melba appeared to be fumbling around in her purse while Chase let himself into his room.

Part 6

Melba waited a full five minutes before knocking on Chase's door. He answered the door and curtly said, "What is it now, Melba? Make it quick because I'm going to bed."

"I think I slipped my keycard in your jacket when we got our rooms," she said. "I didn't have my purse out so I just stuck it in your pocket and then I forgot until I couldn't find it. I'm sorry." She walked into his room and closed the door.

Melba mustered tears in her eyes as she sadly looked up at Chase and said, "Chase, please don't be mad at me. I'm only worried about you. I don't want you to look like a fool if Paula is cheating on you, that's why I got so upset." She threw her arms around Chase's neck and tried to pull him into her for a kiss. Not just a friend's kiss.

Chase yanked her arms away from around his neck, opened the door, and told her to get out.

"I need my key," she said.

The rooms were large with big bathrooms. The closets were off the bathrooms, separate from the bedrooms. Melba took this chance to go to the Cpap machine that Chase had already set up. She slipped the small medicine bottle out of her pocket, opened the water reservoir on the Cpap machine and poured the contents of the bottle in it. She rushed to the middle of the room again just as Chase was coming out with her keycard.

"Don't you think we need to talk about it?" sobbed Melba.

"Oh yeah, we need to talk alright. But we will be talking with Paula present," said Chase. "She needs to know just what her 'best friend' has been up to." He used air quotes when he said 'best friend.' "Goodnight."

Back home, Paula decided not to go out for drinks with the rest of the class. She had this strange feeling of some kind of dread, and she could not identify it or shake it. This feeling nagged her all the way home. She decided to go directly to bed and try to sleep it off. She felt particularly lonely for Chase so she grabbed his pillow and propped herself up to read her book. Within five minutes her book dropped from her hands as she fell asleep. The vision came incredibly fast. It had to be a vision because she had just closed her eyes. She could not have been asleep long enough to dream. Paula sat straight up in bed, wide awake, and looked at the clock. It read 10:00.

She bolted out of bed. The dream again, only this time she saw everything. The woman was clearly recognizable. It took her just about 30 seconds to realize what she saw and what she needed to do, and fast. She hopped out of bed, grabbed her phone and tried calling Chase's cell phone, no answer. She tried Chase's hotel room and again, no answer. The third call was to the hotel's main desk. Luckily it was Gary on the desk and he had talked with Paula on several occasions so they were already acquaintances. Gary seemed pleased that Paula had called and started to ask her how everything was going but Paula knew this was no time for pleasantries, so she interrupted Gary and said, "Gary, listen carefully, this is an emergency."

Gary stopped talking immediately and said, "I'm listening."

Paula quickly took a breath and said, "Gary, I've tried calling Chase's cell phone, and his room, and he isn't answering. You have to go to his room, let yourself in, take his Cpap mask off his face and call 911. But first, transfer this call to your cell phone so I can go with you. Do it now Gary!"

Gary took the elevator to Chase's floor, listening to Paula the whole way. When he got to his room he used the master key to enter. Paula was telling him to jerk the mask off his face when Gary let out a little scream. He said, "Oh God, Paula, he's all swollen!"

Paula yelled, "Take the mask off Gary! He is having an allergic reaction. Go to the bathroom and get an EpiPen from his toiletry bag."

"Okay," said Gary, "I have it. What do I do now?"

Paula calmly but quickly gave him directions on how to use it. After the injection had been administered she told him to call 911 for an ambulance and the police. "Gary, is he breathing? Please God tell me he's breathing!"

Gary's phone was on speaker so Paula could hear that he was calling 911. When he had given them the information he turned back to his phone and said, "Paula, he's breathing but it's very labored." He could hear Paula crying on the other end. Chase heard his wife in distress and his eyes snapped open. He called out to her.

Paula heard his voice and answered, "Chase, I'm here, I'm here."

Gary had been so hyped up on adrenaline that when he heard their exchange he nearly collapsed. He calmed himself down a little, enough to ask, "Paula, how did you..."

Paula jumped in before he could finish and said, "Gary, you have to do something else for us please. When the police get there tell them my 'best friend' Melba tried to kill my husband. She added unrefined peanut oil to the water in his Cpap machine. There is either a little container in Chase's room or she took it back with her to her room. They need to check for that."

"I will," answered Gary, "But Paula how on earth do you know this? You are hundreds of miles away?"

"I guess I just love my husband, and I knew this was life or death," sobbed Paula.

To which Gary added, "More like wife or death I think."

CLAIRVOYANT

---◆◆◆---

Part 1

Her high school overnight dance had a hypnotist and that is where she became fascinated with hypnotism. She majored in psychology in college and finished her four-year degree in three years. She knew in order to become a licensed counselor she would need to further her education but she was too anxious to start counseling. Her future was not clear to her yet but she was not worried. If she was not happy, she would pursue her doctorate but right now she was going to test the waters with the knowledge she had. Without the doctorate she knew she could not have her own practice but she was young and that was a very real future possibility. Then she got lucky, very lucky.

A retirement village was looking for a counselor. Barnwell Retirement Village had a population of over 800 people. She interviewed, and got the position. To be honest, after four months of looking for a counselor, there were only two applicants. The pay was not the best and most people did not want to work at a retirement village, much less live at one. No matter, she got a starting place, and her own little cottage like apartment.

Her first day on the job there was a little 'welcome' meeting for her in the cafeteria. She introduced herself and shared what she envisioned. She said, "Hello everyone, I'm

Claire Voyland, the new counselor here at Barnwell Retirement Village. I look forward to talking to you. Remember that there is nothing that you cannot talk to me about, whether you have a concern or you just plain feel like talking, please come to me, my door is always open." She was worried that nobody would welcome her but her fears were laid to rest when she was approached by at least 20 people right after her little speech.

The next few weeks were somewhat bittersweet for Claire. She was happy because she had more clients than she could have ever imagined but this was also sad because these people all had problems. Fortunately, she was equipped to help them. Most of them just needed to talk through their problems and Claire was a great listener and sounding board. She was able to pull from them what needed to be said or thoughts that needed to be out loud. These were the easy ones but some were not so easy. People who needed help with weight loss and/or smoking cessation were not easy. Of course they had heard it all before, all the reasons for improvement, both medical and personal. Claire had nothing new to offer them, except hypnotism. She always told her clients that hypnotism does not work for everyone and because of this it was still up for debate, but she believed that it was a solid solution more times than not.

Claire knew that hypnotism was still somewhat controversial so she had to approach it carefully with each client. She believed in it wholeheartedly, which made it easier when she talked with the clients. She told them that there were absolutely no side effects, except for the behavior changes they requested. If it did not work, nothing bad happened, they would just have experienced a relaxing session. They trusted her already and to see that she believed in it made them feel safe. She started with clients wanting to lose weight. While they were under hypnosis she basically told them the same things they had heard before, about portion control and how they should feel full after a fraction of what they normally eat and blah blah blah, but now it was different. Now it actually worked.

After one month Claire's overweight clients enjoyed a 90 percent success rate. Out of 20 clients, 18 had successfully lost weight. The percentage would have been even higher but one client started gaining his weight back after two weeks. This was a test base for Claire. All of the clients were only given one session, she wanted to see how long one session would last. Now she knew that repeat sessions, or boosters, would be needed for some clients as reinforcement. Ten of the original 20 clients did not think they needed a booster yet but the others agreed to them. Each individual was different. For some clients, they needed reinforcement every week, but for most it was between three weeks to a month. After another two months, Claire had 95 percent success with her weight loss. One client simply gave up.

Claire was ready to tackle smoking cessation through hypnosis next. This would be handled differently. The sessions would be dependent on each person and could be once a week, once every two weeks, or maybe even days apart. She would need to wait on this to actual measure any percentage of success and even then she would need to trust the clients to be honest with her. After only one week though she was getting accolades from some ex-smokers.

Claire approached the subject of group therapy with some of her clientele to see the reaction and it was unanimously agreed upon. It was during one of these sessions that she was unofficially renamed ClaireVoyant. The session participants all agreed that during their individual appointments Claire was always able to see the futures of each individual and help in ways nobody else could.

The owners and every other boss at Barnwell Retirement Village were all happy with Claire and saw how all the residents loved her. They learned that all her clients were calling her ClaireVoyant because she was helping almost everyone. After only four months the owners rewarded Claire with a bigger office, with a waiting room, and a bigger salary. They also gave her the okay to see clients outside of the Retirement Village. This was especially rewarding to Claire, it was like having her own practice. Like hanging out her own shingle.

Claire was happy there, and very busy. She was especially happy because she was able to practice her much loved hypnotism. She had such a diverse practice that she was never bored, then she met Harry.

Harry had lived at Barnwell for a little over a year. He had diabetes for most of his life and recently had his left forearm amputated. Harry was hesitant when he entered Claire's office. He said, "I don't think you can help me, this is probably something that nobody can help me with."

"Please have a seat Harry, and tell me what's on your mind," said Claire.

"I've read everything I could find on amputee's and what they experience," said Harry. "I know that some people feel phantom pain in the long-gone limbs but that's not exactly what I'm feeling."

"Tell me what you're feeling, Harry."

"I feel silly but you have a kind face, a very non-judgy face," he said, "I'll try to explain it. I know that my hand is gone but I still feel it. It's not pain, it's like I go to grab something and it feels like it's working. Of course, it isn't but it sure feels like it."

"How long has it been since you lost your arm?" asked Claire.

"Three months, so you'd think I'd be used to it by now. I just found out that I'm getting a prosthetic next week, maybe that'll help. I probably should've cancelled this appointment when I got that news, but I forgot so I came in. I wanted to meet you anyway," said Harry. "My wife has been seeing you for weight loss and she looks great now. She feels great, too. You've been all she can talk about since then. ClaireVoyant is what she calls you." He snickered at that last statement.

"Oh, that's wonderful," said Claire, "I'm so glad she feels better. So would you like to reschedule after you have your prosthetic, or is there something you think I can help you with now?"

"I just wonder why it still feels like I can touch things with my hand. I can feel it. I can feel the texture, if it's soft or hard, or even furry. I can feel the temperature of something, a cold can of beer or a warm cup of coffee. I can feel all these things like I'm really touching it but I'm not because my hand's not there. It's like the other night I tried to use my absent hand to pick up my can of beer, but of course I couldn't. It really felt like I could do it but my invisible hand just went right through the can."

Claire was bewildered, "Tell me Harry, I don't know anything about prosthetics but when you have one, you can't feel the things like your real hand, right? I mean the way you are feeling them now, can you?"

"I don't think so," answered Harry.

"Since you are getting yours next week I want you to try it for a couple days. Get it all worked out on how to use it. Then, if you still feel things the way you are saying, come back and we will try a real session," said Claire. "Let's make an appointment for you next week, two or three days after your prosthetic. In the meantime, I am going to do some research myself and we can compare notes."

Part 2

Over the next week Claire read everything she could about amputation and prosthetics. She read about the many issues that amputee's have and what they have tried for relief. She found that many of the concerns were psychological which was completely understandable considering what they had been through. She gained a lot of respect for those who overcame their disability. Now that she had more information she felt she could possibly help a client with an amputation and was anxious to see Harry again.

Five days after he received his prosthetic Harry went to see Claire again.

"I've been anxious to see you again Harry," said Claire, "Have you mastered your prosthetic yet?"

Harry looked at it and said, "Well, I wouldn't say I've mastered it, but it does work. It still feels alien though."

"Are you able to feel with it? I mean like you said you could with your phantom hand?" asked Claire.

"Nope. But what's interesting is that I can still experience that when I'm not wearing the prosthetic," Harry answered. "And to be perfectly honest with you, I'm more comfortable without it but I know I need it. I thought maybe you could help with that. Make me more comfortable with it than without it, I mean."

Claire thought about it and wondered how she could do that, what she could suggest to him under hypnosis. She agreed to try and said, "Okay, let me hypnotize you and give you a suggestion. I don't know if it will work but we can try."

Claire put him under her spell and spoke to him about transferring his feelings when he touches things, over to his prosthetic so that he will still feel them. She suggested that he would feel more comfortable with his prosthetic but she had no real idea how to help him.

After the session Harry was anxious to see if he was more comfortable with his prosthetic so he reached for the bottle of water on the table. The hand found the bottle but from his reaction it was clear that he did not feel it. He looked at Claire and said, "I don't think it worked."

Claire told him to remove his prosthetic and see if he could still feel it with his phantom hand. He removed it and reached for the bottle then with a sad look on his face he said, "I feel it. I feel the cold of the bottle as I grasp it, I even feel the condensation on it."

Claire shook her head and said, "I'm sorry Harry, I tried to help you but I don't think I can. I'm sorry. I don't thi..."

Before she could finish the bottle fell off the table and rolled toward Claire. They both jumped. She looked at it, then looked at Harry and said, "Did you do that?"

Harry looked just as puzzled as Claire when he said, "No, I don't have my prosthetic on. How could I do that?"

"Did you knock it off with your phantom hand?" asked Claire.

"I don't know. I mean, yes, it felt like I was touching it right before it fell, but that hand is not there anymore."

"Pick it up," said Claire.

Harry reached for it with his right hand and Claire stopped him. "No. Pick it up with your left hand, the one that's gone," she said.

He kind of snickered and said, "How can I do that Claire? It's gone."

"Dammit Harry, pick it up!" Claire said.

"Okay, okay," said Harry. He bent over and with his left hand, the hand that was gone, he picked up the bottle. The bottle appeared to be floating in air as he raised it. With his mouth wide open, and a readied scream in his throat, he dropped the bottle, and what sounded like a very loud gargle he said, "What the fuck?"

"Exactly what I was thinking. Pick it up, Harry," Claire commanded.

He reached down again and picked it up, with no hand. With his right hand he unscrewed the top and the bottle went to his mouth. Not to his chin or to his nose, but directly to his mouth. They were both staring in shock, with dropped jaws, at what was happening. He took a drink, then screwed the lid back on and set the bottle back on the table. He looked at Claire and they both started laughing hysterically.

The laughing subsided a little and they both looked at each other and started howling with laughter again. "How can that be? How can I do that? How were you able to do that to me?" asked Harry almost screaming.

"I don't know how that happened," said Claire.

"You have special powers," said Harry. "That's what it is. You gave me back my hand somehow."

"I don't have special powers," snorted Claire, "maybe you do! And I didn't give you your hand back, look, it's still gone!"

"But it's not! I mean, you can't see it but look!" He picked up the bottle again and tossed it in the air and caught it, all with his left hand. The hand that is no longer there. "I don't need the prosthetic anymore. Wait until people find out what you can do!"

Claire screamed, "No! Harry, No! You can't tell anyone about this! Besides, we don't know if it was something I did or if you were already able to do this."

"I wasn't able to do this before today, I tried. It was all you Claire," replied Harry.

"Either way you can't tell anyone, at least not yet," said Claire. "Don't you see what might happen? You might be labeled a freak or I might be labeled some kind of witch or something, and people will hate me, regardless of the fact that it is a good thing that happened to you. Maybe I triggered something already inside you. I just wanted you to be comfortable. Please don't tell anyone yet, until we figure out what it is that happened. I record all my hypnotism sessions, let me listen to that again and see if I can find anything. Right now, you have not even been here. We never had any sessions. You may have to 'rediscover' your hand in front of other people, maybe your wife and kids. Will you do that for me, please? Can you make the pretense as real as it was today? At least try? Maybe not right away though, let's wait a while."

Harry looked at Claire and finally understood what she was saying, "I get it now. Even though what you did was totally amazing, with people the way they are in this world some of them could try to make it out as some kind of black magic and make you evil. Believe me Claire, there is nothing evil about you or what you did for me, but I see what you mean. Isn't it a shame that we can't just announce this to the world? Don't worry. When the time comes, after you have researched more, I'll rediscover it at home, just like here. I'll knock something over while someone, I guess my wife, can see I was an arm's length away from it, but thank you. Thank you so much for this."

"I don't know if it's a blessing Harry. I'm afraid it's going to raise a lot of questions. You will be an anomaly. Maybe even a freak. The man with the invisible hand. I think you better just rediscover this in front of your wife first, but let's wait on that. What kind of reaction will she have? Would she take it as a blessing? Could she possibly keep it secret? I'm not trying to tell you what to do Harry but I do know your wife. Then again, she might think the same thing and not want you going around showing people what you can do. On the other hand, this gift of yours might make for a good magician act if you want to take it on the road." Claire chuckled at that last comment. "Just give it a lot of thought before you decide what to do and remember that we are in this together, even though we know this is a great gift, it most likely will not be perceived as such and one, or both, of us is going to be labeled."

Harry was confused. He was amazed and happy but he understood what Claire meant when she told him to think hard before doing anything. He was mad that he had to even think about it because it was a blessing. Why should he worry what people would think or do when he had the use of his hand back? That is totally screwed up that anyone would have to worry about repercussions in getting the use of your hand back. That sucked. He knew that Claire was right, he had to be careful. He also knew that his wife would be the first one to spread the word. She meant well but she could not keep a secret to save her soul.

Part 3

Harry kept his secret but all he did was think about what could, or would, possibly happen if he revealed it. He played out each scenario and there were times when the scenario did not end happy. He was a freak. Did he bring this on himself? Or was Claire the freak? Did she do this to him? Then he decided they needed to try this on another amputee before they did anything. He called Claire.

Claire had been going over all the recordings of her sessions with Harry and there was no voodoo involved. She was convinced that nobody would find anything religious or even medical with her sessions. Harry convinced her that she needed to have the same session with another amputee, one that knew how to keep a secret, and she agreed. Harry had been to several amputee support group meetings and one person stood out in his mind. Her name was Lilly. She had been in an accident and lost her right leg, all the way up to her thigh. The reason she stood out to Harry was because she was always positive. This was particularly amazing because she had almost lost her husband in the same accident. She had a lot to be bitter for but she refused. Lilly had two teenage girls and she wanted to set a good example for them, and she did.

Lilly wore her prosthetic every day. It was extremely uncomfortable but to be able to walk without help was worth it. Harry had made a lot of acquaintances at his support meetings but he made a real friendship with Lilly. They were both thankful that they were able to wear prosthetics but unlike some of the others in the group, they never felt comfortable with them so Harry pulled Lilly aside after group and told her about Claire. He did not tell her what he was able to do, just that Claire made him feel better somehow.

Lilly and her husband had dinner with Harry and his wife. Despite the age difference they had a great time together. Harry told Lilly that after he saw Claire he was more comfortable wearing his prosthetic and now he wore it always. Lilly admitted that as soon as she got home she removed her prosthetic and hopped around the house. He suggested Lilly see Claire so she made an appointment.

Claire requested that Harry introduce her to Lilly so that she may feel more comfortable. She asked Lilly if she could still feel things with her phantom leg, like water, or temperature change, because Harry said he could still feel things with his phantom hand. Lilly said that she could but she had read that was normal for a while after losing a limb. They chatted a little then Claire asked Lilly to join her in her office. Lilly was hypnotized and Claire gave her the same suggestions she had to Harry. Affirmations about feeling comfortable with her prosthetic, feeling like it was truly a part of her. She had listened to the recording of her session with Harry numerous times so she used the exact phrasing.

Harry was in the waiting room when Claire and Lilly walked out together.

Harry was the first one to speak he said, "Lilly, I know you're going to think I'm crazy but please just do a couple things for me."

Lilly looked at him strangely and said, "Okay, what do you want me to do?"

"Okay, first," said Harry, "I want you to watch closely." He took his prosthetic off and with his invisible hand he picked up a bottle of water. Lilly was staring at the water bottle flying in the air. Then Harry set the water bottle down on the table and put his hand on Lilly's arm.

She screamed when she felt his hand and yelled, "What the fuck! Harry what the hell is going on? What is going on with your hand? Is that your hand?"

Harry patted her with his invisible hand and said, "Yes, Lilly, that's my hand. The hand that I lost. You can clearly see that I don't have a left hand anymore, yet, I'm touching you with it. Now, I want you to do one more thing."

Harry looked at Claire and then back at Lilly and said, "I want you to take off your prosthetic and try to walk. Claire will be on one side, and I'll be on the other so you won't fall. I know this sounds crazy but please just try it. Try it for me."

Lilly trusted Harry but she thought this was a little crazy. Harry supported one of her arms and Claire the other as Lilly started removing her prosthetic. As soon as it was gone she fell over on Harry, who was supporting her missing leg. She said, "Harry, what the hell did you think was going to happen? This is just sick." She started to cry a little. "Why would you do this to me?" She straightened her left leg in an effort to stand and as she did, the trash can standing next to Harry was knocked over. There was nothing near it. They all looked at it. "I felt something with my right leg. I felt it kick that trashcan but that's impossible, right?" She looked at Harry first, then looked at Claire, "Right?"

"Try standing up," said Claire.

Lilly bent her invisible right knee and put her weight on it. She stood up. She cried out "I'm standing on my leg that's gone!" Then she just cried, cried out loud with long weeping sobs. Claire and Harry hugged her. It was a crying huddle.

After almost a full minute of the crying huddle, Claire and Harry stepped back and looked at Lilly. Lilly was looking at her leg that was not there, yet she was standing perfectly straight. She took a step on her right leg while still holding her hands out in case she fell. She was not yet fully trusting of the invisible leg. Harry and Claire also had their arms out so she could grab hold if she needed, but she did not. She was walking with two legs but only one was visible. It looked very bizarre. It looked so bizarre that Claire jumped back and said, "Oh no! I just realized something guys. It's for sure now that you can't go out in public without your prosthetics!"

"What do you mean?" asked Lilly, "This is fantastic! It's a miracle!"

"Yes," said Claire, "It is a miracle! I agree! But look how unnatural and strange it looks. Especially you Lilly! Walking perfect with only one leg, you'll be labelled a curiosity, or freak, and I'll be labelled a witch."

"But it's more like a miracle! It's a really great thing!" cried Lilly. "I can't thank you enough for what you've done for me! I love you Claire! I love you Harry!"

"Claire's right," said Harry, "We'll be freaks and she'll be a wizard of some kind. People will get a lynch mob together for Claire, despite the great thing she can do."

Claire looked pensive as she said, "Also, whatever I said to you, it worked on you both but it might never work again plus, we don't know if this is only temporary, it may not work tomorrow, or next week! I know that you wear shorts a lot but for Lilly it would be easy to cover up by just wearing long pants. I know that your prosthetics are uncomfortable but maybe you can take out the guts and just have sort of like a shell so that it looks like the prosthetic. Harry, you could wear long sleeves but gloves would be a little odd, since it's always warm here, maybe driving gloves or maybe some kind of paint? I don't know, I'm just trying to brainstorm. I really think we have to see if this is just temporary and keep it to ourselves, at least until we can figure out something out."

"I don't think we can do that yet," said Harry, "Like you said, you don't know if this is only temporary but if we had fake prosthetics on and our magic died, then our prosthetics wouldn't work. It wouldn't be so bad for me but for Lilly that would be a travesty. And if it is only temporary, would another session with you make us whole again?"

"Claire, you look like your deep in thought," asked Lilly, "what are you thinking?"

"As much as I hate to say this, what if it was just a fluke with both of you?" said Claire. "I don't mean....."

"It's definitely not a fluke," interrupted Lilly, "If you have to give it a title, let's call it a miracle, plain and simple, whether it's temporary or permanent, it's still a miracle! Wouldn't it be something if our invisible limbs became visible again? We know that Claire did this, maybe that can happen too!"

"I'm sorry," said Claire, "I'm certainly not making light of your situations. What I mean is, let's say this is permanent, let's hope this is permanent, but if it is, it's going to get out there. You guys are not going to want to continue wearing prosthetics if you don't need to, and nobody would expect you to, but it will get back to me. Even if you guys didn't say it outright, they would explore your background to see that I was what you had in common. Now, that would be great if I knew that I was the answer for all amputees, but who knows if it will work again?"

"So is it that you're afraid that this won't work on anyone else?" asked Harry.

"Well, yeah of course, there's always a chance of that but if I can, what the hell are they going to think I am? Even though we know it's a wonderful thing you know they're going to label me some kind of witch or demon or maybe even alien but it's going to be something bad," cried Claire "Hell, you know that. Sometimes people can be such fucking idiots that they don't take the good for what it is, they have to find something bad!"

Lilly looked at Claire and said, "Okay, well for starters, I can assure you that Harry and I would never point to you, if that's what you want. We would discover our miracles in front of family and be just as surprised as they will be."

"You know," added Harry, "If you're scared you can't make another miracle, I'm sure that Lilly and I could find another amputee that we could trust, right Lilly?"

"Oh yeah, sure!" said Lilly. "We have a lot of good friends in our group and every one of them would be so happy, just like Harry and me. I think just about any one of them could be trusted if they could have this miracle."

Harry jumped up and said, "I know what we can do!"

Lilly and Claire both stared at him and said, "What?"

He said, "Lilly, you know Mark, in our support group?" She nodded. "Well, he works at the prosthetics lab department. He's like an engineer and designs them." Harry told them a little about Mark.

Part 4

Mark was a young engineer who had climbed quickly in the

prosthetic engineering department. His bosses were so impressed with him that they had already given him his own department. He was a single, handsome, engineer who only had eyes for his job at this time much to the dismay of many female admirers. His bosses loved it but they knew someone would catch his eye sooner or later. Regardless, he was an engineering wizard and they knew he would go far. Because he was an amputee was unfortunate for him but he could use himself as a guinea pig on new things and give an honest answer.

In his senior year at college, Mark had taken a part time job at a mill where a machine had malfunctioned and took his hand. He refused to sue but the billion-dollar company insisted on helping him. He no longer had to work to finish college. He no longer had to work period. He was now a millionaire, five times over but he was still a working man and had no intention of stopping.

Harry told Lilly and Claire what he knew about Mark. He knew how he lost his arm but he did not know about the millionaire part. Mark was not a braggart.

When he finished Claire said, "Oh, I get what you're saying. We see if my session will work on him and if it does he can design fake, comfortable prosthetics, right?"

"Yes," said Harry. "That way, if God forbid, this is only temporary and we lose the use of our invisible limbs, we can blame the prosthetic we are wearing. Also, we would see if your magic will work again on a third person, Mark."

Claire smiled and said, "Okay, lets table this until our session with Mark. You guys talk to him and ask him to come and see me. I want you both to be here for the support I need. We will do it just like Harry prepared you Lilly. Anyway, I have to get out of here I have a date and I'm already late."

"Who are you seeing?" asked Lilly.

"Dr. Arthur Lasser. I guess you know him Harry, he's a doctor here at Barnwell Village. I've been seeing him a few months now."

As she was walking back to her apartment Claire saw Art's car pulling up to the front door of the medical building. He got out, opened the passenger door and helped a lady out of the car. It was one of the nurses that worked at the medical building. He engulfed her with a hug, then a kiss. It was not an air kiss, like a good friend. It was a kiss smack on the mouth, like a lover. Claire told herself to calm down, her and Art had not talked about exclusivity yet so it was none of her business. She knew she would fit something in about it tonight during her dinner with him.

That night Art and Claire went to a nice restaurant and Claire nonchalantly asked Art how his day went. It's one of those questions nobody really cares about the answer, it's just a courtesy of sorts, but this time Claire did care about the answer.

"Same as the day before and probably tomorrow," answered Art. "Sometimes I get tired of sick people." He laughed a little, "I guess I shouldn't say that because that's why I get paid. I guess I think it would be nice to see people who are not sick for a change."

"I think you saw one person that was not sick today," volunteered Claire. "At least she looked pretty fit when you dropped her off at the medical building."

Art looked up quickly and dropped his fork at hearing Claire say that. He stammered a little as he leaned over to pick up his utensil and said in a very demanding voice, "Um, what are you getting at Claire? What are you accusing me of?"

"Getting at? Accusing you of? This isn't an inquisition Art, I just stated a fact. Why are you so upset? We have never talked about being exclusive," said Claire.

"No, well, yeah, um well, I want it to be exclusive," stammered Art.

"Oh, you mean now? Not starting yesterday or this afternoon but starting right now?" asked Claire.

"No, I mean I've wanted us to be exclusive from day

one. Today wasn't anything. We didn't do anything," said Art.

"I see," said Claire. "Maybe then we need to talk about what exactly exclusivity means to each of us. To me, it would mean that kissing another woman, the way you kissed her today, would be outside the boundaries of exclusivity. Now if you think that your actions today are inside the boundaries that could be a problem."

"Okay look," he started, "I went out to lunch with someone that I had been seeing, before you of course, and I told her today that it was over."

"So, that was a goodbye kiss?" asked Claire.

Art looked at Claire with pleading eyes when he said, "Yes, Claire. That's exactly what that was. Before you and I started dating I dated her for six months but I broke it off with her three months ago. She just got back in town and I guess she forgot we broke up but yes, that was a goodbye kiss."

Claire decided to leave it alone because whether it was a goodbye kiss or not it was not her business since they had not established their relationship earlier. Now though, it was exclusive. That issue dropped and their evening went on without incident, at least no incident that evening.

Now that Claire and Art were exclusive that meant that they had a standing engagement for the weekends, unless one of them had to work. Art never had emergencies, there were other doctors that covered the weekends for him, but Claire did have emergency calls on occasion. On a normal weekend they went out to dinner on Friday, went back to Claire's apartment and Art stayed over. Saturdays were intended to be another date night and Claire would have loved to spend another day and night with Art but her work sometimes interfered.

Harry, Lilly and she had spent time together going over their options and her upcoming appointment with Mark, the prosthetics engineer, who unfortunately was out of town on business for three weeks. They knew they needed to keep their secrets for longer but everyone agreed.

Things were going well between Claire and Art, for awhile. One Saturday, Claire had originally had an appointment with a client who needed a boost with his non-smoking and it could not wait until Monday. The client called right when his appointment was supposed to start and he was very apologetic but he needed to cancel, his boss needed him that day. Claire never got mad at her clients because she knew shit happened but she was a little upset that she missed spending the day with Art. She decided she would take a detour to his house before going to her apartment and surprise him. She not only surprised him but she surprised the nurse that was with him. He stammered and stumbled and tried to come up with something but they both knew that he had just screwed the pooch, or the nurse in this case.

Part 5

Claire was surprisingly calm as she went to her apartment. She could not believe her own mood. She felt happy. She guessed that she did not have anything invested in her relationship with Art after all. Oh, she was still mad at him for being an asshole, but she was relieved somehow. Then she figured it out. She was relieved for being out of a relationship with that asshole.

She fixed herself a drink and sat down to watch a movie when there was a loud commotion in her yard. Her neighbor was out there with a chainsaw cutting on the shrubs and trees that separated the two yards. It appeared as though he had absolutely no reasoning behind his destruction. She ran out to stop him. She yelled, "What the hell are you doing?"

He turned off the chainsaw and said, "I'm cleaning up some of these weeds and shit."

She scowled as she shot back, "Those are not weeds you moron! They are shrubs. They were planted specifically, and you are taking perfectly good branches from a perfectly good tree. Stop this insanity immediately!"

That got him a little upset so he growled as he said, "Well, I don't see anything stopping me from doing this. Especially not you, missy!"

Claire may have been a little more upset with her earlier confrontation than she thought because now she was fit to be tied. She stared at her neighbor and he stared back. During this time Claire gave him a little suggestion as she glanced back and forth from his eyes to the hand holding the chainsaw. Suddenly, he dropped the chainsaw and screamed. He looked down at his hand as if it was alien to him. He looked at Claire and said, "Help me, something happened to my hand."

Claire ran over to him and helped him to the porch of his apartment. She asked him what happened and he told her all the sudden he had no control over his hand. "Should I call for an ambulance?" she asked. "Did you maybe cut yourself somewhere?"

The neighbor's wife ran out to the porch yelling all the way, "I knew you would hurt yourself using that damn chainsaw! I told you you'd cut yourself!"

He answered, "No, I'm not cut anywhere. All the sudden my hand just let go of the chainsaw. I can't move it."

Claire put her hand on his forearm and said, "Do you feel my hand?"

"No."

Claire put her hand on his arm right above the elbow and asked, "Can you feel my hand now?"

"Yes, I can feel that. It's like my arm is numb from the elbow down, I can't move it," he said.

"Sounds like some kind of nerve damage to me. I'm calling an ambulance. You need a doctor to look at it," she said.

His wife followed as the ambulance took him away and he was thanking Claire for all her help but Claire knew exactly what happened to his hand. She was going to have to fix that but it certainly answered the big question. It was Claire.

It was always Claire. She had a gift. Maybe it was not a gift though, maybe she was a demon or a witch or something else evil. *Oh God*, she thought, *what if I'm evil?* This was the first time she had ever wronged somebody. Or was it? Had she caused havoc before and not known it? No. She did not believe that and she knew that tomorrow she would right the wrong against her neighbor. She would get rid of that chainsaw first though.

She did not have to wait until the next day to see her neighbor again. They drove home after only two hours at the hospital. He started walking over toward her. She locked eyes with him and made a little suggestion again as she glanced down at his useless arm. As he approached Claire she asked, "Well, what is it?"

He said, "They could not see anything wrong, they are going to run more tes....." Before he could get the last word out he looked down at his hand and it was moving. He was moving it. "Well, I'll be damned." He wiggled his fingers. They were not moving as fast as he had commanded them but they were moving. "My hand is working!"

Claire said, "Oh God that's great! What did the doctors say?"

"They had no clue so they took blood but I guess I need to call them now and tell them it fixed itself."

Claire looked at him and added, "You might want them to go ahead and run those tests on your blood though. Maybe it was just a fluke, but then again maybe there is something." As soon as she said that word fluke, she realized she had used that word on several occasions lately.

He nodded and said, "You're right. I'll let them go ahead and test for anything out of the ordinary but I'll let them know that I have a little movement back. Thank you again Claire for taking care of me. I'm sorry about the chainsaw and all, I was mad about something else and was taking it out on the bushes. I'll leave them alone."

"Thank you," said Claire, "Have a good evening."
He nodded, "Right back at ya Claire."

Part 6

On Monday afternoon Mark walked into the waiting room and was immediately greeted by Harry and Lilly. Mark looked a little pensive as Lilly walked over and locked the door behind him. She said, "Mark, you're looking at me like we have something bad in mind for you. Believe me, this is not the case, besides, you were the last appointment of the day." Then she called out for Claire.

Claire had been going over her notes in the office but when she heard Lilly she came to the door to meet Mark. "I've heard a lot about you Mark, it's so nice to meet you. Lilly and Harry were talking about you and the support group you all attend."

Harry knew Mark better than Lilly did so he added, "Mark, first let me say that this is absolutely no reflection on any prosthetics you may have engineered. We are both happy we have them but Lilly and I came to Claire because we had not been amputees for that long and we had trouble accepting our prosthetics. We just could not get used to our alien additions."

"I remember that you and I had a similar conversation. Of course nobody believes that a prosthetic of any kind can completely replace our missing part but most people get comfortable with them. Just like me, you lost your left arm, from the elbow down, and around the same time. Anyway, we brought you here because Claire has been able to make us much more comfortable and we wanted to see if you felt the same. That maybe you could be more comfortable too. Are you game?"

Mark looked at Claire and said, "I'm absolutely game. Why the hell not! Like Harry said, I know we should all be thankful for prosthetics and nobody wants to sound like a cry-baby because we have to use them. We should thank our lucky stars that there is such technology but that doesn't mean we are good as new. They will most likely always feel alien so of course I would welcome a chance to feel more in tune with my prosthetic."

"Okay then," said Claire. "Mark would you please join me in my office?"

"Yes," answered Mark, "lead the way."

As soon as they went into the office and closed the door Lilly quickly said, "I get to talk to him about it when he gets out! I called it!"

Harry laughed and said, "Okay, you can talk about his reveal but you have to be careful about it because it might not have worked for him. We still want to keep this secret so we have to make sure that it has also worked on him before we reveal anything, right?"

"Right," she answered. "How do we do that? So first we ask him to remove his prosthetic, right? Then what? How did Claire do that with you?"

"It was really just an accident with me, at least at first." said Harry. "I had my prosthetic off and I knocked over a water bottle with my ghost hand. Then Claire told me to pick up the bottle and when I started to reach for it with my right hand she yelled at me. She told me to do it with the other hand. She saw it before I did, I guess. It was pretty amazing. So, I don't know how we can approach this with Mark."

"Maybe you could just put your ghost hand on him," volunteered Lilly.

"Or maybe you could just take your prosthetic off and walk toward him," said Harry. "That would freak him out."

"Wait though," said Lilly, "we want to see if his works first or our secrets are out."

"Shit," said Harry, "why don't we just see what Claire does. I think she's the smartest of us."

"Okay, yeah, you're right," said Lilly. "It will be better coming from Claire anyway. Oh, God, I hope it works for him."

Claire had Mark sit down on the couch and put him in a hypnotic trance. She was already sure that her 'suggestions' would work on him too. She was certain because she knew that she was not only capable of bringing the amputated limb back, she could also make a limb useless. It was still there but the person could not use it. She proved that with her neighbor when she 'suggested' his arm was gone. She still had to be careful what she said. She gave Mark the same suggestions that she had given Harry and Lilly, then she woke him up.

Mark looked at her and said, "Is that it? Are we done?"

"We are done, Mark," replied Claire. "Do you feel rested?"

"Yes, I do. Thanks for that," said Mark.

"Does your prosthetic feel any different to you? Any different at all?"

"I was going to say no to that question but now that you've mentioned it, I don't know, it's odd but it might feel a bit more cumbersome than usual," said Mark. "I've gotten so used to it that it normally feels like my new appendage, but it feels a little more alien now for some reason. No, no, no, that's not right at all, I think I'm just imagining it since you said something."

Claire walked over, opened the door to the waiting room and waved Lilly and Harry into her office. Mark was sitting on one end of the couch. Claire said, "Mark, things may get a little crazy from here on out but it's nothing bad. Would you please remove your prosthetic?"

"I don't mind saying," replied Mark, "that it is a little unsettling with you three just staring at me."

"I'm sorry," said Claire, "Right now, just pretend they are not here."

Mark removed his prosthetic as Claire walked over to the couch. He looked up at her and said, "Okay, what now?"

"Hold your phantom arm up," said Claire, "Like you were going to 'high-five' me."

Claire reached her hand out in the air at precisely the

point where Mark's real hand would be. Then she grabbed his hand and intermingled her fingers with seemingly nothing, but she felt his hand and he felt hers.

"Holy fuck!" cried Mark.

"I think that was exactly what we both said when it happened to us!" said Harry.

Mark took his other hand and put it over Claire's hand. They stood there looking directly into each other's eyes for what was a very uncomfortable moment for Harry and Lilly.

"Hey guys," said Lilly with a little giggle in her voice, "We're here, remember us?"

The connection between Mark and Claire broke and Claire took her hand away leaving Mark's two hands together. He kept feeling his ghost hand with his other hand and he laughed a little as he said, "Claire, what have you done to me? Have you made me whole again?"

"We aren't certain what I have done," said Claire, "is it a blessing? I don't know, your hand is still gone but yet it's there. We weren't sure if it would work again but if it would Harry and Lilly said you would be the perfect person and I'm glad they chose you."

Part 7

Harry went over to the mini fridge, grabbed a bottle of water and said, "okay, well, let's show him the full effects of your magic sessions."

He took off his prosthetic and used his ghost hand to drink from the bottle. Lilly removed her prosthetic and walked around the room. That looked really odd.

Mark looked quite odd himself as he was seemingly moving only one hand in front of him when he was moving both but he actually stopped to stare when Lilly walked toward him with only one leg.

"I kind of feel like I should be in the center ring with a top hat on right now," cried Claire, "but it's wonderful!"

They all laughed. Big gut belly laughs all around.

Laughs with tears. Afterward, they all sat down while Lilly got out the bottle of champagne she had brought and she passed out cups filled with bubbly.

Mark proposed a toast, "I want to thank Harry and Lilly for bringing me to Claire, for more than one reason, I might add."

Claire blushed and added, "I agree whole heartedly."

Mark said, "Okay, so we do look as if we belong in a freak show but I believe I know why I was the one chosen."

"Mark," Lilly volunteered, "yes, you're right, you were chosen because you engineer prosthetics but believe me if we had known you this well before, we would have chosen you anyway. And I speak for everyone when I say I'm so glad we did!"

Claire and Harry nodded in agreement.

Harry added, "We took a chance that you wouldn't be an asshole. If that had happened, Claire would have had to take back her suggestions and leave you alone."

Mark laughed and said, "So glad I passed! I know exactly what I need to do and I'm already working it out in my head. We all need 'fake' prosthetics so we can walk around like normal. I can make something that looks as if it has some plastic parts on it. For Lilly, it can be like tights, skin colored but enough to show that it is not real skin. The tights themselves will have these parts that look like plastic but they will be comfortable. The same for Harry and me. I've already got some prototypes in my head. First I'll need measurements from Harry and Lilly and a dinner date with Claire. These are my only conditions."

Everyone looked at Claire. She blushed a little more as she took another sip of champagne and nodded.

"I'm famished," cried Lilly, "Let's all go over to that little taco stand down the street. We need to suit up though first," she added as she picked up her prosthetic leg. "We can talk, have some tacos, some margaritas? Si?"

"Sounds good," said Mark. He put his prosthetic arm on then laughed and said to Claire, "This is not the official dinner date though."

The four of them ate tacos, drank margaritas, talked and laughed. It was trivia night at the restaurant so they paid to join. They came in second and received a free meal and a small plastic trophy. Their four brains worked together like a well-oiled machine. When the trivia match was over they began brainstorming on their new prosthetics. Mark had it almost entirely worked out already. He said, "I have a lot of material at home, seems I'm always trying new things since my own accident. I may be able to come up with something comfortable that we all like. This could be the start of something big," then he looked right at Claire when he finished his sentence, "and the start of a beautiful relationship," he quickly looked at both Harry and Lilly too and said, "between the four of us I mean."

They laughed because they knew exactly what he meant. Then they got quiet because they were probably all thinking the same thing but Claire said it aloud, "So, I know Mark is probably thinking, well, maybe all of you are thinking, why should we keep this secret? It's a good thing, yeah? Of course it is, but will it ever happen again? Chances are good that it will. Is this forever? That's the question that's in my head."

"Exactly," Harry said, "We know that this is a wonderful thing that Claire can do for amputees but will it last forever? And if we announces this to the world what would happen to Claire? Especially if the use of our ghost limbs goes tits up after only two months, would her magic work on us again?"

Lilly said, "Yes, we have just been thinking about how wonderful this has been for us but if word got out it I'm afraid it would not be wonderful for Claire."

Claire shook her head and said, "I'm so thankful that I can do this for you guys, I mean, I'm genuinely happy for you. What I'm mostly thinking about is the time factor involved. Hopefully it is forever. If that's the case, and people all know, will I be able to help more or will I be damned in the public eye and treated like a leper? I know that I don't have to tell you that people can be very cruel to someone who is different."

Mark then joined the conversation, "I get it. We all get that. I think there's maybe a way to avoid that and there may be a business venture in it for us." That got everyone's attention. "I will make us some comfortable prosthetics while we sit tight for a while. Then if we are still using our ghost limbs, after three months or so, that would be your call, we bring one more person in to see Claire. We know she has the power, we just don't know if it's a forever thing. We then make her or him another fake prosthetic. As time goes on we could possibly be making many fake prosthetics and that could be a business for us. Of course we would only charge a fraction as much as the real prosthetics because they wouldn't be real prosthetics, they would be more of a cosmetic item but definitely something that people would want. Plus, if our ghost limbs gave out at any time we could always blame it on a faulty prosthetic."

Lilly added, "You know it might be a situation that we would never want to announce it to the world but do you honestly think it will be kept secret for long? The way I feel now, and especially after Mark makes our devices, I would never tell anyone and maybe the next amputee might not but they will tell their families." She looked around and added, "I know that my husband will find out even if I didn't tell him. I've been avoiding him for a couple days because I know he will feel my leg, I have to tell him so he doesn't find out accidentally. I trust him completely, he will never betray me. My other family members are also completely trustworthy, that would be my dogs and my cat."

Everyone agreed to the trustworthiness in pets.

"Okay," said Harry, "We all agree that we need to protect Claire so let's set a date in the future, maybe two months, and if we are all still experiencing this magic that Claire has bestowed, we will invite another person to see her. There are a lot of people in our support group. We can keep going and try to get to know some of the other members even better so we can decide. Does that sound like a plan to everyone? And Mark, I agree with your plan on starting a business and I already know what we could name it. We would name it HF prosthetics. HF would be the initials that stand for the first two words out of each of our mouths after Claire gave us our limbs back."

Everyone nodded and laughed. Lilly was laughing as she said, "I have to get home to the wife and kids." Harry agreed, his kids were also his pets.

They paid their bill and rose from the table. As they stood up Mark's hand brushed against Claires and she felt a bit of shiver, a good shiver. He felt it too, even through the unnecessary prosthetic he wore.

They stopped outside the restaurant to say their goodbyes. Harry and Lilly left and Mark walked Claire to her car. He reminded her, "Remember, I said this was not our official dinner date."

Claire nodded and said, "I do recall something like that. I'm free this weekend, but instead of going out, how would you feel about coming over, kicking your shoes off, watching a movie and ordering in?"

"That sounds great," he answered. "I'm looking forward to it." He bent down to give her a kiss on the cheek but he missed and got her right on the lips. He missed on purpose and she reciprocated. He waited until she was buckled in the driver's seat with the engine started before he walked to his car. He turned and waved as she drove away.

Part 9

Claire was excited about everything that transpired at the restaurant. She was excited about the future. She could see that they genuinely wanted to protect her and she knew she had made some lifelong friends. She smiled as she drove until she got to her cottage. Art was sitting on her front porch. She parked in her driveway and walked to the porch with her keys in her hand. Art got up to meet her at the door.

"Go away," she said, "We have nothing to talk about. I have nothing to say to you and there is absolutely nothing I want to hear from you."

"No, no, no, now honey, you need to listen to me," he pleaded. "You don't understand at all. She had just stopped by to tell me something."

"Please leave," said Claire. "I don't want you here, I don't want you around me at all, anymore. We are done, Art, we are done."

"Claire, sweetie, you're not listening to me." Art was almost pleading now. "You and I are still a thing, nothing has changed. You don't have to worry, you are still my number one!"

"You egotistical asshole," Claire snarled then she looked him right in the eye. Art thought this was a good sign. He thought everything was going really well because she just kept talking to him calmly and looking him up and down. He could not understand her words, she was talking quite soft, almost like a murmur, but the whole time while looking deep into his eyes he could not help but notice her frequent glances at his crotch. He knew he had her just where he wanted.

GNOME MAN'S LAND

$\leftarrow\!\!-\!\!-\!\!-\!\!-\!\!\blacklozenge\blacklozenge\blacklozenge\!\!-\!\!-\!\!-\!\!-\!\!\rightarrow$

Her husband had been gone for ten years now after almost twenty years of marriage. Gertrude had been happier in these past ten years than she ever was in the previous twenty. She did not miss him and would have been even happier if he had left twenty years ago. Needless to say, it was not a marriage made in heaven. He strayed.

Fortunately, their daughter Diana, was away at college when Gertrude caught her husband of nineteen years cheating on her. That first time he was caught he said he was so sorry, and it would never happen again. "I don't know what came over me," he said, "it was her fault, she was all over me. Blah, blah, blah," too many possible excuses. "This was the only time it ever happened," and "Men are different than women," he would often tell her, "We have these urges that have to be satisfied. Women don't have to worry about them. It's really a curse." Gertrude did not believe any of that nonsense and she knew that he was only sorry that he had been caught in a lie. She was not stupid, but she was terribly naive.

Six months later she caught him again. This time she saw it with her own eyes. She came home from work early and heard a commotion in the guest bedroom. Her husband jumped to the door as she opened it. The window was open, the screen was out, and the curtain was flapping in the breeze. She could tell that his little feeble mind was trying hard to come up with something believable. It struck her as funny and she laughed as she walked through a cloud of cheap perfume and picked up a polaroid picture, lying next to a cheap tiara, on the dresser. She stopped laughing as she looked at the picture. It was sad. A twenty-something, unkempt girl, naked from the waist down, sat on the edge of the bed, that very bed in Gertrude's guest bedroom, with her legs spread. A smile on her face that showed two missing teeth and the cheap tiara on her head. Gertrude guessed that the tiara was a prop from her husband. He was a real gem.

An envelope hidden in the bottom drawer of the dresser held at least five more polaroids of different girls, in the same pose, with the same tiara and the same sad smile. Gertrude helped him pack his bags, including the tiara and polaroids, that night. He tried calling several times but after the divorce was final Gertrude told him she never wanted to think of him again. Diana was eighteen years old and it was her decision if she wanted to continue a relationship. Gertrude's only rule was he could never be at the house. Diana met him for lunch one day but then she never heard from him again and she was fine with that.

These past ten years without him have been wonderful.

She had been in the same house for thirty years. A few renovations and now the house was absolutely perfect. The yard had always been perfect. Gertrude had a green thumb. She lived at the end of a cul-de-sac with a wooded area behind her large yard. Her side yard was large as well and this was where she planted her vegetable garden. Flowers lined her side fence. In her back yard were several old oak trees and three flower gardens. Flowers lined her back fence and in one corner, where the flowers from the side yard met those in the back, there was what appeared to be a large tree stump, but it was actually a house. It had a large door, windows with shutters, and a roof. A house for her gnomes. Gertrude loved her garden gnomes. They had been with her for years. In fact, her oldest friends had been with her for over thirty years. They were Gunther and Klaus. She was very young when she fell in love with garden gnomes. She learned everything she could about them.

Garden gnomes were first produced in 19th century Germany and made of clay (resin and plastic by the 1970's). Originally called Gartenzwerge or garden dwarfs, gnomes were known as a symbol of good luck used to watch over crops and livestock, sometimes tucked into the rafters of a barn or placed in the garden. Gertrude often thought that maybe she did not possess a green thumb, maybe her little friends were responsible for such beautiful bounty.

Gertrude read everything she saw about garden gnomes but in the end, she liked to apply her own stories to her little friends. Gunther and Klaus, she imagined, were like the fathers of her little clan. They were the only two that were made of clay. Because she felt they were very wise, she would discuss any problems she had with them. Gunther was special. She did not buy him, he appeared in her flower bed when she was young. She never really questioned it, she always told herself that he chose her. Of course, all her gnomes were more than happy to help her with any problems, but she had a special bond with Gunther.

The neighborhood had once been amazing. Everyone living on the cul-de-sac had been there at least fifteen years so everyone had seen the children grow up and most of them were delightful. Gertrude's daughter, Diana, grew up with a lot of friends and there were always a group of kids at the house. Gertrude took an active part in helping with the neighborhood kids. She babysat, baked cookies, and helped getting the kids on and off the bus, when needed. The neighbors loved her, and the kids loved her more, except for one, Damon. The children were welcome in her yard as long as they respected her plants, animals, and her gnomes. Damon was the only one who made fun of her gnomes, and Gertrude made a point of watching him closely when he was there.

Damon was okay until he turned around seven years old, when he got a slingshot. Over the years he began to alienate all the other children until he no longer had friends. The other kids called him Demon, instead of Damon, and that was fitting because he would shoot anything with his slingshot. He had become proficient with the weapon and the neighbors would see dead birds or squirrels or any other poor animal that came near Demon. Frequently, cars would have cracked windshields or mirrors, streetlights would be shattered, and mailboxes were often battered beyond repair. Everyone knew that it was Demon but could not prove it. Even if they could prove it there would be no reprimand for the seven-year-old. Demon's mom was long gone, and his dad was a drunk.

Then came the morning when Gertrude walked out and saw Gunther.

"OH NO, OH NO, OH NO!!!! What happened! Gunther, your head is cut!" There was a big chip off the top of his head and if someone had not known that he was made of clay, the red inside the chipped part could have passed for blood. It even looked moist. She looked around and found the chip lying beside a rounded rock that had no place in her garden. She knew immediately what had happened. "That little fucker! I want to make him hurt like he hurt you!" She picked up Gunther and the chip and with tears flowing from her eyes she ran into the house. "I can fix you, don't worry I'll fix you," she said between sobs. "I know I can!"

Gertrude carefully carried Gunther to the table and sat him down. She took the chip and fitted it back on him. She felt relieved when she saw that it had not shattered beyond repair. "I will fix this, sweetie, I swear, you'll be good as new, I promise." She was happy when she had the chip back in place and it appeared almost perfect again, but she was not at all happy that it happened. Gertrude was not easy to anger but cruelty drove her rage. Cruelty to animals or to her little friends. Demon was guilty of both, and he must be punished.

Later Gertrude carefully carried Gunther back to the yard. There was a tiny chip from his red cap missing but a little paint took care of it. Demon never bothered the gnomes again.

Her daughter, Diane, finished college and moved to the city but visited regularly. Every week as she pulled into the driveway she could see her mother's yellow straw hat among the flowers. The neighbors said that when they saw a bright yellow straw hat in the garden they would yell a greeting at which the hat flipped up to reveal Gertrude's smiling face.

After she retired, Gertrude was a fixture in her gardens. She missed work but she loved being able to spend all day in her gardens with her friends. She talked to her gnome friends all day. All the neighbors accepted this and did not think she was odd at all for doing it. In fact, when neighbors visited, they also greeted the gnomes. Gertrude had them convinced that gnomes were good luck. After all, she had the biggest, juiciest vegetables and the most beautiful flowers.

She would tell them stories about her little people and how they were around in ancient Rome. How they lived underground, where they would guard the nearby plant life, and their own stashes of buried treasures. Her neighbors figured she either had the most excellent imagination or the stories were true. Either way, they were most entertaining. She would tell them that gnomes were just like people, they loved to talk, tell stories and play. They are mostly active at night though, when people are less likely to see them move.

Most people loved hearing about the gnomes and believed they brought good luck. Several neighbors had purchased their own gnomes and believed they were enjoying beautiful gardens because of it. The newest neighbor, Mrs. Peabody, did not like gnomes. She did not like anything. She kept her BB gun full to shoot at any squirrels or birds that came near her. Other than Mrs.

Peabody and Demon the neighborhood was great.

Gertrude assumed that Demon must have moved away and after a few complaints about Mrs. Peabody, she never shot anything again. It was perfect there now.

As the years passed, Gertrude hated to admit it, but she knew her time was running out. She talked to her gnomes now all day and she could not identify if they were talking to her or if she was making up the tales they told. She did not care. One of her favorite tales was of a spot in the forest not far from here where they go, via tunnels, when they are not with her. It was a wonderful, safe life there with an entire community. They told her, or so she thought, that they liked her and that when she was gone they would disappear from here too. Gunther asked Gertrude if she would like to join them.

Diana was stopping by twice a week now to check on her mom. She was worried that she would soon be unable to live by herself. That morning, she went to see Gertrude only to find her in bed. The ambulance was too late, Gertrude was gone. She passed quietly but not without asking Diana to promise she would go outside and tell her gnomes goodbye for her. Diana knew how she loved her gnomes but that was still a little strange, it was like her mom was trying to tell her something, or maybe show her something. She kept her promise and walked out into the garden. She immediately noticed that Gunther, usually a solitary gnome, was now holding hands with a female gnome wearing a bright yellow straw hat, both wearing big smiles.

The next day, in preparation for the funeral arrangements, Diana sadly went to Gertrude's house. She was immediately drawn to the yard. She knew that her mom fabricated all those tales about the gnomes, right? They could not be true, right? Regardless, she had to get a better look at that gnome with Gunther. That was a new gnome and she was with Gunther. They had both looked very happy. She had to get a better look.

The gnomes were gone. All of them. She was mad at

first, thinking they had been stolen but these neighbors would not do that. She walked over to the gnome house in the corner thinking maybe they were all in there but when she lifted the roof she saw a hole, or rather like the mouth of a tunnel and lying next to it were three items. A cheap tiara, a slingshot and a BB gun.

I LOVE MY MOM

◆◆◆

My mom is the best. She takes care of me. I think I have some kind of disorder. I went to school for a while but now I'm home schooled every day, well, not every day. Some days I get a little wild.

I might have some kind of disorder but my mom has never hit me or even yelled at me. She is very patient with me. When I was even younger she took me to the park to play with the other youngsters at least once a week. I loved it. We played ball and sometimes a game called tag for hours. I wore myself out. Maybe that's why Mom took me to the park so often because when we got home I would be too exhausted to get into anything.

Like I said, I think I have some kind of disorder. I don't mean to do things wrong, I just do sometimes. I know I'm just six years old but you'd think I could give myself a bath by now. I can't but that's okay because I love for her to give me a bath. She gets my hair all suds up then sticks it straight up from my head and she just laughs. Even when I look funny like that she still tells me I'm the prettiest girl in the world. I really like that. I love my mom.

I told you I think I have a disorder. My older brother is very different from me but I love him. Mom loves him too. He goes away every day for school. I watch that yellow bus come and pick him up every morning and I get so excited when he comes home. He doesn't pay as much attention to me as Mom does though. He has other friends now that I guess are more fun than me. They play out in our backyard. I know I'm just a little sister. He used to let me play ball with them but now I don't do that very often anymore. I still love him and I know he still loves me, I'm just not as much fun as his other friends now. I know Mom loves him because she does the same thing to him as she does to me. She puts her hands on each side of his face and tells him he's the handsomest boy in the world. Then she kisses him on the forehead, just like she does to me only when she does it to him he makes a face. I love it though when she does that to me except she says I'm the most beautiful girl in the world.

I spend most of my time with Mom anyway. She reads to me and we watch TV together and have snacks. Sometimes she throws the popcorn up and she catches it in her mouth. She's pretty good at it but I'm better.

She knows when I don't feel good and I know when she doesn't feel good. No matter though she always has time to talk to me and kiss me. When she does that I just wag my tail and kiss her right back.

I'M SORRY

"Look, I said I was sorry, that's all I can do," he said. "That's not good enough anymore," she answered. "You always do this. You have always done this. You do what you want then when you apologize you know I'm going to accept it. It's erased. Clean slate. At least in your book it was erased and you could start over but not anymore, and never in my book. Your words don't even have meaning to you. When you say you're sorry, you don't really mean it. You're just saying it because you believe that it's what I want to hear. I don't want to hear anything from you anymore, especially not those words. As of this moment right now you have my blessing, not that you ever needed it, to do anything and everything you ever wanted with impunity because we are done."

"Aw, your ass," he said.

"And that is always your response," she said.

"Well, I don't know what else I can say," he said. "You said my apology didn't mean anything anymore so what the hell am I supposed to say?"

"Well, for starters, why did you cheat on me?" she asked. "Do you honestly believe that an apology will erase that? Are you only apologizing because you got caught? How many times has this happened?"

"Why are you bringing this up again. I told you I never cheated on you. I know you don't believe me but I swear I didn't," he said.

"You're right, I don't believe you," she said.

"Besides, that was years ago," he said.

"So you have just admitted that it happened, but it shouldn't count because it was years ago," she said.

"I didn't say that but yes you should just shut up about it," he said.

"I have proof and you know it. Proof of at least one time you cheated but it's really hard to believe that it was the only time. And because it was years ago doesn't count. I was just too stupid to see it then. I was too trusting, too in love, and far too naive to see it and realize you were just a lousy cheater. I wasted a lot of years on you after that because I was stupid so that's on me. But no more," she said.

"What's that supposed to mean?" he asked.

"We're done. I want you to leave. We'll sell the house, split it, and go our separate ways. If you don't want to leave, I will. I don't want to ever hear an apology out of your mouth again, it means nothing to you and nothing to me. I think though that I owe you an apology so here's my apology. I'm sorry you're an asshole. I'm sorry I didn't do this years ago. I'm sorry that I wish you were out of my life forever," she said.

She walked over to the door, opened it and stood aside so he could pass through. As he walked by her he started to say something but she just shook her head and he stopped. He walked outside and she closed the door.

She cries. Not because he left. Maybe because she felt stupid. Maybe because she could have had a totally different life if she had recognized him as the bastard he was while she was still young. God damn her naivete. God damn her humanity for even crying at all.

About an hour later she senses something outside. She goes to the door to see him walking up the steps. She steps aside as he walks in. He is bleeding from the head and chest. His clothes are torn and tattered. There are cuts and bruises on his arms and his face.

"What happened to you? Are you alright?" she asked.

"Yeah, I'll be okay in a little bit." he said, "I'll be okay if you will forgive me. I know I have been an asshole. I know I'm guilty of everything you said to me. I would say I'm sorry but I know how you feel about that so instead, I'm asking if you could ever forgive me? And before you answer, I want you to think about it, I mean really think about it, because I do love you, and I really am sorry."

"For some misguided reason, I believe you really mean what you are saying, this time anyway," she said. "But too little, too late. You knew what you were doing to me for all these years and I just can't justify erasing the entire past because you may actually be sorry this time. You can't just 'I'm sorry' it away any more. Please leave."

She is still standing at the open door as he passes to leave for the last time. She watches him walk behind the tree in the driveway as a siren is heard in the distance. The siren gets louder as the police car stops in front of her house. An officer climbs the steps, identifies himself and tells her that her husband has been in a fatal accident about an hour ago. He looks at her and says, "I'm sorry."

LIFE IN PICTURES

Part 1

She was looking for a particular size picture frame.
Aside from her many pictures, her life was empty. If
she had the right frame she could finish her collage
and let her mind wander through it. It felt almost good, at
least for a while. Most of her pictures included images of
her 'family' at the foster care facility where she grew up. She
had only two pictures of her parents. One was on their
wedding day and the other was taken on the day they were
killed in an automobile accident, when she was ten years
old.

After looking in most of the shops in the downtown
area, Cameron saw an ad for a big antique shop. She figured
she just as well check it out so she walked past the little
shops and diners to the huge Victorian house at the end of
the lane.

It was a beautiful house with an antique shop on the
main floor. She looked through the window of the shop and
noticed a lot of picture frames. She was not looking for an
antique frame, she was looking for a cheap frame, but since
she was looking for an irregular size, she thought she might
as well go in and see if maybe there was an inexpensive
frame that was a fit for her. She was looking only at the
larger ones, not quite poster size but larger than most
photograph frames. She whipped out her measuring tape

and started measuring.

The older lady near the stairs was intently watching Cameron's every move. It was obvious the customer was looking for a specific size frame, but the older lady was more interested in what she saw in the woman herself. She had studied people for years and had yet to find another person who was special, like her. This customer was the first to get her attention so she decided to investigate further.

Cameron had yet to find the perfect size when an older lady approached her. "I help young lady?" asked the older lady.

The sound of her voice hit Cameron like a familiar friend. They had never met before but there was something about this lady that Cameron was instantly drawn to, she felt an immediate bond, a mysterious pull, like a magnet. The older lady had a strong accent and very broken English, but for some strange reason, it sounded like home to Cameron.

Cameron looked at her and smiled. The older lady wore a red vest over a white puffy blouse, a handkerchief skirt and small hoop earrings. She looked like someone you would meet to have your fortune read. Gypsy came to mind but Cameron remembered reading somewhere that it was no longer politically correct, she hated that because she loved the name Gypsy. Not many people could pull off this look but somehow it worked for her and the look matched the voice perfectly.

"I am Agrapina," said the older lady, "I'm to help you."

Cameron held out her hand to shake and smiled as she said, "Hi, I'm Cameron, so nice to meet you."

As the ladies shook hands Cameron felt a surge of electricity pass from Agrapina. It was not like a static electrical shock; this electric was not an accident. It felt good. It felt empowering for Cameron somehow. It was over in a split second and Cameron wondered if she had imagined it.

Cameron quickly said, "Oh, I'm sorry Agrapina, did I

shock you just now?"

Agrapina smiled and replied, "No dear, no shock. Was real, what we had. We alike, Agrapina and Cameron." When she spoke she pronounced her w's like v's and she rolled her r's.

"What do you mean, do you mean we have something in common? Is that what you mean?" asked Cameron.

"That's it. Not felt that for years. It's nice, huh?"

"Well, I don't know. How are we alike?"

"We have sight. Can see what others cannot. Can do what others cannot. Special."

"Agrapina, I don't think I'm special at all."

"You are, just not yet. I teach. You look for picture frame, right?"

Cameron looked surprised at first but then she remembered that she had been measuring frames so the lady must have seen her. She answered, "Yes, I have a specific size in mind but I can't afford an expensive antique. I thought by chance, you may have one in here that wasn't expensive."

"No worry to you. I have what is needed."

"Agrapina," said Cameron, "that's an interesting name. Where do you come from Agrapina?"

"I am here from Romania," answered Agrapina, "In my country, name is for girl born feet first and we are blessed. Can see what others cannot, can hear what others cannot."

Cameron looked at her surprisingly and said, "I was also born feet first."

"I know this," said Agrapina, "You have sight. You have gift."

Cameron shook her head and said, "I wish I did but I'm just normal."

"You have gift. I help. You see," answered Agrapina. She gave Cameron a big smile. Cameron noticed she had a beautiful smile with whiter teeth than you would expect in an older person but with teeth just crooked enough to prove they were her originals.

The only other customer in the antique shop was ready to buy something so Agrapina told Cameron to wait for her. She walked over to the register where her and the customer exchanged pleasantries then she rang her out and the customer left. Agrapina walked the customer to the door and when she left Agrapina changed the door sign to 'closed' and locked the door. She walked back to Cameron and said, "We talk, eh?"

Cameron felt a little anxious when Agrapina locked the door. She was not scared but she felt like she should be. She looked at the door and back to Agrapina and said, "What're you doing? I'm a little scared right now."

"I know Cameron. I know she not scared. Several years for someone like you I've waited. You know to be safe with me, you know in heart, you safe," said Agrapina.

Oddly enough, she was right. Cameron knew she should be scared but she was not. What made her anxious was the fact that she was so comfortable with this lady that she just met. She looked at Agrapina as she said, "You know, I should be very uncomfortable with what just happened. You, a perfect stranger, just locked me inside alone with you."

"Oh, not perfect," Agrapina laughed, "not stranger either. Deep inside, Cameron knows me. When hands touched, Cameron felt connection, this is right?"

"I know I felt something," replied Cameron, "I don't know what it was, it's never happened to me before."

"It was the sight," answered Agrapina, "we connect over powers we have."

In a whispered voice Cameron said, "But I told you, I have no powers."

"Until now, no powers," said Agrapina, "I awaken them, now I teach you."

"Agrapina, I'm not sure what the hell is going on right now. I only came in for a picture frame and now you're telling me that I have some kind of special powers? It's a little overwhelming, for sure."

"We go upstairs to home," interjected Agrapina, "we take shoes off, drink Tuica, maybe a bite to eat, and we acquaint each other, yes?"

"I don't know why I am even still here," said Cameron, "normally, I would say no way to an offer like that but for some reason I feel I have to do it. What is Tuica?"

"Ah, drink from Romania, is from plums, so good for you, right?"

"Right."

Part 2

Cameron was blown away by the living space upstairs. It was like a museum but still cozy. The wood carving in the furniture, doors, and ceilings was unbelievable. Cameron hated modern houses with modern furniture and this was as far from modern one could get but still had all the amenities of a modern house. It was absolutely gorgeous. Agrapina sat down, kicked off her shoes and pointed to a small couch across from her, for Cameron. Cameron sat in the plush comfortable couch she was pointed to, took off her shoes and immediately felt like she had grown up here. This could be home for her easily.

A huge parrot flew up and landed on Agrapina and said, "Hi gorgeous!" He gave her a kiss on the cheek and said, "I love you."

Agrapina kissed it back and said, "Love you too. Meet Cammie, new to family, say hello."

The bird looked at Cameron and said, "Hello."

"Hello. You are beautiful," Cameron said to the bird.

"I know," said the bird.

"Ehh, you not be so cocky," Agrapina said to the bird. Then she looked at Cameron and laughed as she said, "He knows is beautiful, guess I make him cocky."

Agrapina had placed a bottle of Tuica and two glasses on the coffee table between them, she pours, and hands one to Cameron. She appears to study Cameron a little and then says, "Is gorgeous, I know. You love, I know. Is home to you already, yes? Is comfortable for you. You losing apartment, you move in with me, okay?"

Cameron looked shocked as she said, "How did you know that? How could you know that? I just found out today."

"I know. I learn much when we connected. I have much to teach for you. Drink Tuica, delicious, help to relax. Sit back, you home now. We need each other. Plenty to talk about, but now we rest." said Agrapina.

It was too much for Cameron to understand right away. She felt torn. On one hand she wanted to get up and run away as fast as she could, but the other hand was winning. That other hand told her to stay and drink and relax and do whatever Agrapina said. Cameron sipped the Tuica. It was delicious and it warmed her all the way down to her bare feet. Agrapina was right, it helped her relax. With one more small sip every problem in her mind faded away, and she had problems.

At forty years old Cameron had lost her job when her company was absorbed into another and her services were no longer needed. It was only then that she realized she should have been planning ahead. She was lucky that she had been with the company for so long time with no college degrees or real experience but she never dreamed she would be out of a job.

She had lost everything. No pension, and soon no apartment, the only thing she wanted to do was make a collage of her happier times. In her heart she knew this would solve nothing and instead she should be looking for another job, possibly in the fast food industry, but right now she just wanted to put her happy times together, with a big collage, and get lost in them. A collage scattered with photos of happier times. Pictures of her friends in the foster facility, but only two pictures of her parents.

Those thoughts were all washed away now either because of Agrapina or the Tuica or both. If it was the Tuica then that was some good shit.

"Cameron, I wash away your problems," said Agrapina. She pointed to the staircase leading downstairs to the antique store and said, "You work here now." Then she waved her hand around her head and said, "You live here now. We are fast friends. You will like."

Cameron did like.

"We go downstairs, I show you around while store closed." said Agrapina.

Agrapina had finished her tour when a large German Shepherd came inside the shop from the huge back yard. He came right up to Cameron and gave her a little kiss on her hand. Cameron squatted so she and the dog were at face level and pet him. The dog started nuzzling her and pushed her into a sitting position on the floor where she was quickly overtaken by another dog with a cat right behind. She was in heaven. They were all trying to get her attention and she was loving every bit of it. She laughed as she said, "Where did all these guys come from?"

"Live here," said Agrapina. "Not as friendly with customers so stay out of view. They like you though, know you family."

"I love them all!" cried Cameron, "Animals are so much better than humans!" She hugged them all individually and was talking to them like she had known them forever.

Agrapina pet one of the dogs and said, "Okay, we all love later. Go upstairs for dinner now." She headed toward the stairs with the animals in tow. Cameron brought up the rear. Agrapina prepared bowls of food for each animal and set them on the kitchen floor. She put the bird's food in a container on his stand. The animals all ate from their assigned bowl.

Agrapina fixed a quick dinner for her and Cameron. "We rest now, come in TV room with comfy chairs." With plates in hand, Agrapina led Cameron into yet another room that Cameron had not seen before. It was almost like a movie theatre room but much cozier. There were tables beside each chair where Agrapina set their dinners. Then she turned on the big screen TV, cracked open a bottle, filled two glasses, then plopped down in a chair.

"More Tuica?" asked Cameron.

"No, no, that's for special. Wine for dinner. Good wine," answered Agrapina, "we enjoy dinner, movie, wine. Big day today for my Cammie. Relax."

A movie started and the animals came in and made themselves at home. One of the dogs climbed in the plush chair with Agrapina while the other one joined Cameron. The cat lounged on the back of Cameron's chair and the bird perched on the back of Agripina's.

When it was time to retire for the night Agrapina got up and told the animals to go get their business done before bed. They had a doggie door that led out to a huge fenced yard so they all ran out quickly. When they returned they were torn. Normally all of them would go directly to Agrapina's bedroom to sleep but now there was another member of the family. Cameron's room was also very large with a king size bed so she would be more than happy to have any roommates. There were bird perches in every room of the house so he floated wherever he wanted. The other animals all went into Agrapina's bedroom at first but before she fell asleep, Cameron had a dog in bed with her.

Part 3

The next morning Agrapina fed the animals then fixed breakfast for the humans. Cameron woke to the smell of breakfast after the best night's sleep in years. She dressed quickly then joined the rest of the family in the kitchen. The animals went over to say hello and Agrapina said, "Good morning my Cammie. Eat, we have busy day."

Agrapina set the plates on the table and sat down across from Cameron. "We move you this morning, then I teach you something I have much need for help with and you have gift. Can help. Already you can run store but this service is what only you or I can do."

The morning was devoted to Cameron moving from her apartment to Agrapina's house. It took less than three hours total. It was only as she was packing that Cameron discovered how little she actually owned. Her most prized possessions were her pictures. While gathering all her pictures, Cameron thought she must still be in shock. She wondered how she could be moving into a perfect stranger's house but her wonder about it was quickly shot down. Somehow, this was right, she was not at all in shock.

Her pictures reminded her of happier times. Cameron's mom and dad were killed in an accident when she was young, so at ten years old, with no other family, she was put into the foster care system. She spent most of her time in the state facility since people were looking for much younger children.

She had pictures of the other kids she knew at the foster facility, several people in all those pictures were deceased. The only two pictures she had of her parents was one of them on their wedding day and one taken on the day they died. Of course she wished her parents had lived but she did make some good friends during her foster years. Those years she compared to years in prison. It really was only one step up from juvenile detention. The only redeeming quality she found was her friendships.

Fortunately, the apartment was furnished when she moved in, so she had no furniture to move but that was also unfortunate because she realized just how little she had in life. Some clothes and pictures of the past, enough to fill four boxes. Cameron found herself crying as she packed the fourth and last box. She carried them out to the street and started to cry again when she saw Agrapina get out of her car to help load them. This cry was because she was so thankful to have Agrapina in her life.

Agrapina walked over to Cameron and hugged her. As Cameron hugged her back she felt that same electricity pass between them, more subtle this time but it felt right. She wiped her eyes and said, "I can't tell you how much I appreciate you, Agrapina."

Agrapina wiped a tear from her face and said, "We family, you, me, and any animals I adopt because that what I do." She snickered as she said that and Cameron laughed. "Like I say, we family, you call me Aggie, and I call you Cam or Cammie my baby. We family, okay?"

"You won't believe this but my mom's name was Aggie and she called me Cammie. Now I know, this feels good. You're my family."

"Yes," said Agrapina, "We family."

Agrapina's house was big and Cameron's bedroom was bigger than her last apartment. Agrapina went downstairs to open the antique shop while Cameron unpacked. She had more than enough storage for all her belongings. It was strange but she was happy. For the first time in her life she could actually look forward to the future. Whether Agrapina was good or bad it did not matter to her. She felt the connection and she could honestly say that she felt something big for Agrapina. It was almost as if she had a mom again.

She spread some of her pictures on the desk in her room. These were the ones she was going to use for her collage but it was not the biggest thing on her mind right now. Right now she needed to be with Agrapina. She needed to learn whatever Agrapina could teach. She would be the most attentive student ever.

She went downstairs to the antique shop, looked around, then called out "Agrapina?" No answer. "Aggie, are you down here?" She knew she was because there were customers wandering around.

Then Agrapina called out "Cammie, here!" She was pointing out a frame that looked like it would fit what Cameron had in mind. "You take upstairs, do project you want frame for. I be up later to talk to you."

"No, that can wait, it's not as important to me anymore. Let me help you down here. Tell me how I can help you," said Cameron, "remember you told me I had a job so let me earn my keep a little, please, Aggie?"

A huge smile appeared on Agrapina's face as she said, "Yes, Cammie, I show you." She walked Cameron around the store and told her facts about all the items as they walked. Cameron could not believe how much history there was in this shop, and she especially could not believe how much Agrapina knew about all of it. In the past, Cameron would never have been able to retain all the information that was spilling out of Agrapina but now, she was certain she could, and it was all because of the electric connection they shared. It was one of the gifts that Agrapina had given her. This was a feeling that Cameron had never had. It was like she had meaning in her life, she was not completely useless. She was absorbing everything that Agrapina was saying. It was amazing, she was like a sponge, and she wanted more. She was truly interested in all the history of each item in the store, and better yet, she was learning all about them.

A customer walked over to them and asked about an item. Agrapina nodded to Cameron and Cameron began spitting out the entire history of the item. The customer was astonished and wanted to buy the item so Cameron walked her over to the desk and checked her out.

Part 4

When the last customer left Agrapina locked the door and flipped the closed sign over. Cameron followed her and said, "This store is huge and you know everything about every item in here, I want you to teach me." Agrapina nodded.

"Yes, I will, but sometimes people want to know things. Not come to buy items. You, me, we have a sight. I use tarot cards to show things to people. Cards talk to me. Can use other things to see as well. Personal things. A necklace, key chain, anything personal shows me about person who is gone. I answer questions. Able to see things others cannot. People come in to talk with me about their own life. I can see things about their life and you have same gift. You have ability, same as me, just need to awaken," said Agrapina.

"I never saw anything special in me but if you see it then I believe you," said Cameron. "I noticed that you seem to have an overabundance of picture frames though, in fact, that's the reason I came in at all."

"Frames special to me, to you," said Agrapina. "Use for actual visits to my sister and brother, Juliani and Dragos."

"You use them to visit your sister and brother? I don't understand" asked Cameron.

"You see later, biggest gift. Now we close shop, go upstairs, feed animals, rest." said Agrapina.

"You say I have a gift, what gift do I have?" asked Cameron.

"You like me, you have sight. I teach you how to read tarot cards for people who want to see things, or how to see things from personal items they bring. A lot of teaching and learning," said Agrapina. "Finally I teach you about the visits people come for. This very special gift. You see abundance of frames, right?"

"Yes, that's why I came in."

"They help people connect to the past," said Agrapina.

"Well, yeah, that's why people have pictures, so they can remember the past," added Cameron.

"But more. I do more. You will do more. People discover my gift and spread news and others come, so many I turn away," said Agrapina.

"You do something else with the frames?" asked Cameron.

"Yes. Connect live people to their dead through pictures and frames. Has to be both, not one or other," said Agrapina. "People always carry pictures but not always carry frames, so we have plenty here."

"What are you saying? Are you saying these people can actually connect to their dead relatives or loved ones?"

asked Cameron.

"That's it. I use, talk to sister and brother, Juliani and Dragos. They die long ago but through picture and frame we talk," said Agrapina. "I go into picture, I help others go into pictures."

"I don't understand," said Cameron, "Are you saying that you physically go into the pictures by some kind of magic?"

"Yes, body goes into picture," said Agrapina. "I help people visit loved ones long gone, or house of dreams, or vacation spots. Places they can't go in real world. I give them happiness for a while. I show you how, you help people too."

"How long do they get to visit these people or places?"

"Can't stay too long or they get lost in there. Need to pull out, get them back to real world. Fifteen minutes in real life is too long, five or maybe ten minutes is normal for regular customers. Longest I let someone inside was for fifteen minutes but only once, way too long for both of us. She come every week and only for five or ten minutes. She is ready to come back after ten minutes. It wears you out in mind, and them out of breath. Won't do any longer again. Too long. Most people for first time, five minutes, then next time ten, stay that way then. They want more time, they come back," said Agrapina. "Time different there though. Five minutes here in real world is a couple hours there."

"So you have more and more people visiting you for this, right? And it's because of word of mouth, I mean you certainly don't advertise this. Do you charge them for it?" asked Cameron.

"No. No charge, but always they give money anyway. Yes, only word of mouth. Too many people to help for just me. They bring pictures, pick frame, I help to visit picture. They give lots money even though I say no charge, only donations." said Agrapina.

"Okay, how can I help?" asked Cameron. "How do you do this?"

"I show you, just so you see why peoples come back for. You not able to do this for while though. We wait on this. We concentrate on tarot cards and personal items for while, okay?" asked Agrapina. Cameron nodded. "Get picture of someone gone you want to see again."

Cameron went to her room and came back with both pictures of her mom and dad. She held them out for Agrapina to see. Agrapina said, "This wedding day, right?" Cameron nodded. "You not born yet so you no exist. You not in world yet. I think maybe you able to go into picture as yourself now but they think you crazy if you try to tell them truth." When people go in picture, they always are in the time of the picture, not current time, not today."

Cameron handed her the other picture and Agrapina picked up a frame and slid the picture inside. Cameron said, "This was on the day my parents were killed. It was at my babysitter's house. They were going to the bank and only supposed to be gone for about an hour or so but they never came back. They never made it to the bank."

"When you get there, you same kid in picture," said Agrapina. She looked at Cameron and said, "Come, Cammie. Need to hold hand and sit. When I say we come back, you must. No questions. You obey that, right?"

"Yes, of course," said Cameron. "I'll do whatever you say. What do I need to ....." She did not even get to finish her sentence before she felt very dizzy, like she was spinning around the room but she was still sitting on a chair. Then a bright light filled the room and she noticed that she was no longer in the room but outside, in front of her babysitter's house, with her mom and dad.

Cameron hugged her mom and dad so fiercely her mom cried out, "Oh, Lord, you act like we are going to be gone forever! So theatrical! We'll be back in no time, we're just going to the bank. Then we'll come back and get you and go for ice cream. Okay?"

"No, please don't go to the bank!" cried Cameron. "You can do that tomorrow."

Cameron's dad said, "Cammie, quit it. We can't go tomorrow, we have an appointment with the manager today and we're going to be late unless we leave right now. We'll be back in an hour or so, everything's fine."

Cameron was still crying and carrying on when she heard Agrapina's voice telling her she had to go now, felt a tug on her hand. Right now. She had promised that she would go as soon as she heard a call from Agrapina so she told her parents that she loved them. She closed her eyes and let her mind connect with Agrapina. Next thing she knew she was sitting in the chair next to Agrapina.

Agrapina said, "Cammie, you go back in another picture next time, one from before that fateful day, but not now. We rest now."

"That's the only picture I have of us together and I think I could maybe save them, I could talk them out of going to the bank right then. That guy that runs a red light will be gone already and they will be saved! Aggie, I can save them! I can change everything!"

Agrapina sadly looked at Cameron and said, "No change time, Cammie. Ever."

Part 5

Cameron fell over and sobbed. Agrapina threw her arms around her and tried to comfort her. She knew exactly how she felt. Almost whispering she said, "Cammie, know what it feels like, what you feel, I try to save sister and brother but can't. I try to save others, but can't. You find different picture. This one too hard for you. Please believe, won't happen."

"Why not?" Cameron mumbled out in short sobs. "Why can't we do that? It seems like it would be a simple thing."

"It does," sighed Agrapina. "Okay, we go downstairs, open store. I have people coming with questions and some with pictures, I need you help me."

"Okay, I'm sorry Aggie, sorry for breaking down and

sorry for doubting you. How do I do for other people what you just did for me? How do I take them inside the picture?"

"I tell you this later, much later, you do cards and questions for now," said Agrapina. She picked up a tiny squeak toy, handed it to Cameron and told her to concentrate on it. Cameron held the toy, closed her eyes, and tried to concentrate but nothing was coming through. Agrapina touched her hand and said "I give you little boost this time."

Cameron felt a shot of energy when Agrapina touched her hand and before her last word was uttered Cameron's mind was flooded with pictures and videos of a dog playing with the toy. "This is a beautiful, happy, dog. I think it's a chihuahua. She is so happy, running back and forth and playing with the other dogs. This is her favorite toy."

Agrapina smiled and said, "You can see now. You could answer questions about the puppy. You right, she was very happy. One of my babies. Long gone now but not forgotten. This is how you see things when people hand you objects. Mind is flooded with information. You make people happy. I might have to give you little boost at first but soon you get all by yourself."

"We go open now," said Agrapina. They went downstairs. The animals followed and went through to the back of the store where they either relaxed there or went out in the back yard.

There were customers waiting when Agrapina unlocked the door and flipped on the open sign. Some of them started milling around the store but a couple went directly to Agrapina and asked for her special service. She took them to a room in the back and introduced Cameron. Agrapina said, "Is Cameron, my protege. She has same power I do but she no do visits for while, no photos, but she good with cards or sight."

The first lady handed her a picture, Agrapina slipped it into one of her picture frames and called Cameron over. "Cammie, set timer for five minutes please."

After five minutes, they were back. Agrapina held her head for a minute, then shook it off and smiled. The customer was happy, stuffed what looked like hundred dollar bills in the tip jar and said she would be back next week.

Another customer walked back to the little private area and handed Agrapina a necklace. Agrapina handed it over to Cameron and touched her hand sending a little bolt of energy through her. Cameron immediately saw a young woman walking through a meadow. The customer started asking her questions about the young woman and Cameron was able to answer all of them. Then she volunteered some new information to the customer which made her very happy. After five minutes Agrapina took the necklace from Cameron and returned it to the customer.

Cameron was dizzy and disoriented and would have fallen down if she had not been sitting. Her head cleared in a few minutes and the customer thanked her for her vision, jammed a wad of money into the tip jar and said she would be back. Cameron was fully recovered by then and felt amazing. She had made someone very happy and felt blessed that she had that ability. Agrapina had told her that this gift could be very pleasant when they show people good things but sometimes what they saw was not good. That's when they sometimes told half truths to the customers. Agrapina was a kind woman and did not see any real reason for telling the people bad things.

There were two other ladies still waiting back by the private area. Agrapina put her hand on Cameron's shoulder and said, "Cammie, you go help other customers please. I will get these next two ladies." She ushered the next lady in the little back room and took her into her picture. Five minutes later she was back. Then she took care of the last lady.

This went on all day. Cameron was able to use her gift two more times that day but the picture visitation services were all handled by Agrapina.

When closing time came around Cameron was more exhausted than she had ever been from her office job. This was a good exhausted she thought though. Her mind and body were both spent. She was happy about the day. She was happy that she had the power to help people and she would have never known about that if not for Agrapina. She was happy because she had family now.

Agrapina locked the door and turned off the open sign. Cameron slipped her arm through Agrapina's, called the animals, and they all walked upstairs. Cameron fixed the animal's dinners while Agrapina prepared dinner for the humans.

Part 6

Two weeks later Cameron was doing readings for three or four people a day without being exhausted. The more she did them, the less taxing they were on her. She began to realize what people wanted to hear even before they asked and she was able to read tarot cards with ease. She was happy. She had grown to love her new family. Agrapina loved her too but she knew it would not be long before Cameron insisted on trying out picture visitations. She had decided that Cameron did not have the discipline for that so she wanted to keep that from her as long as she could, forever if possible.

Cameron loved her new life and she loved her new family. Agrapina had taken her inside several of her photos and that made her even happier. Since her only photo of her with her mom and dad was taken on the day they were killed, Agrapina tried to talk her out of visiting that one again. She wanted to keep her from hurting and she knew Cameron would try to keep them from going to the bank again but as Agrapina tried to tell her, she could not change things. She knew though that it was only a matter of time.

Another month went by and Cameron felt as if she had been here her whole life. She was helping more in the store and in the kitchen and she felt amazing. For the first time in over thirty years she had a real family. She loved them. Granted some of them were the furry or feathered kind, but they were real, and the best part was that they loved her back.

Another month goes by and Cameron is still enjoying life. Agrapina knew that the day would come when Cameron wanted to learn how to go into the pictures. She could put it off again but Cameron had been so patient and Agrapina felt that she could be trusted with this so that evening after dinner she sat down with Cameron and said, "Is not hard for us physically, just mentally. They have seat, one hand you have on frame, other you hold their hand. Look into picture, concentrate until you see waves, then you just set mind to picture, it's blurry now but then bright light, when it clears, person in picture. Don't let go of hand or they get lost in picture. The body is gone but you still feel hand. After five minutes, you call them back, you still feel hand, pull on it and only let go of hand when they again in this real world. Here you do me." She hands a picture of her sister and brother to Cameron. "This time I won't visit, just in, out, so you see how to do it."

Cameron took the photo frame in one hand and Agrapina's hand in the other. She concentrated on the photo, saw waves like heat, then there was flash of brilliant light, it cleared and Agrapina said "I'm in. Call me back." Cameron called her back without speaking, pulled on her hand that was not really there, and seconds later Agrapina was once again sitting beside her.

"You good?" asked Agrapina.

"I guess, but I have a terrible headache though," answered Cameron. "What if I screw something up? What if I can't do it right? How do you go inside by yourself?"

"That something you not ready for. You concentrate on customers. Just do for five minutes, always hold hand, call back after five minutes. That's enough time. I told you, time different in picture world. Five minutes is like maybe a couple hours there, maybe more. Regular customers I give ten minutes sometimes. Could be like eight hours in picture world but time is cruel master. Time is a thief so they always come back for more," said Agrapina. "Is too taxing for us. Only do couple a day for while. Five minutes max."

"You keep stressing that I have to hold their hand, even though their hand is not really there, what happens if I let go?" asked Cameron.

"Maybe lost forever in picture, you keep hand because your mind goes into picture with them. They don't see you but you see them. You set timer here for five minutes. Your head start to hurt in minutes, when you hear timer you pull on hand to bring back," said Agrapina.

"Would that not be a good thing, being able to stay in the picture with loved ones?" asked Cameron.

"No. Still alive. Picture people not alive. Pictures only one dimensional. Gets hard for living to breathe. I only stay for long as maybe ten minutes our time, but feels like hours in picture. Then have to come back."

"Also, and this very important Cammie, you know butterfly effect?" Cameron nodded so she continued. "When we take people into picture, they do nothing but talk. Any actions, of any kind, would change time, like a person staying, and dying, in picture. Change time because that person dead now in picture, did not live life, change time. Change not only his life but every other life he touched."

"But you can go into the pictures by yourself now, and come back out, will I be able to do that too?" asked Cameron.

"Not soon." answered Agrapina. "Take long time for that discipline. Don't be sad, please remember can't live in past. Living in past, not living. No future for you in past. Future for you in the living. Also I fear you would try again to save parents."

"Yes, you're right. But I promise I won't try that again, I see now," said Cameron.

One afternoon a man came in for a picture visitation. Agrapina greeted him by name so Cameron knew he was a regular visitor. He looked so familiar but she could not place him. He was maybe in his late fifties so he may have been friends with her parents. She just could not place him. Agrapina took care of him that day and Cameron asked about him later.

Agrapina said, "He a regular customer. I see him every two weeks or so. His brother was killed in accident many years back. He brings different pictures of him and his brother. He forgot last picture. Left it here in little room."

Cameron went over to the back room and picked up the picture. It showed two men in their late teens standing by a car. The men looked familiar for some reason to Cameron but when she saw the car she realized why she knew them. That was the car that killed her parents and the man that visited Agrapina was the driver. She knew that car because it was a one of a kind bright green convertible, like no other. Two brothers were in the car. The brother riding shotgun died on impact, like her parents. The driver lived and now he visited with his dead brother every week or so. Cameron knew what she had to do. She would be the one who held his hand next time he visited his brother. She would let go of his hand and wait for at least fifteen minutes to tell Agrapina that they had lost contact. That way if Agrapina tried to go in and rescue him, he would already have suffocated. If he did not exist back then he could not run that red light and kill her parents.

He came back only four days later. It was his brother's birthday so he wanted to visit him. Cameron justified his death with the death of his brother and her parents. If he had not run that red light, he would not have killed his brother, or her parents, so she felt justified.

Her plan worked. As soon as she put him in the picture she opened her hand, pushed him away, and whispered, "Goodbye you useless piece of shit." She allowed plenty of time for him to suffocate, fifteen minutes, before she alerted

Agrapina but Agrapina still tried going into the picture to save him. It was too late.

Part 7

She was looking for a particular size picture frame. Aside from her many pictures, her life was bad. If she had the right frame she could create a collage and let her head get buried in it. It felt almost good, at least for a while. Most of her pictures included images of her 'family' at the foster care facility where she grew up. She had been orphaned at ten years old when her parents were collateral damage in an attempted bank robbery.

After looking in most of the shops in the downtown area, Cameron saw an ad for a big antique shop. She figured she just as well check it out so she walked past the little shops and diners to the huge Victorian house at the end of the lane.

It was a beautiful house with an antique shop on the main floor. She looked through the window of the shop and noticed a lot of picture frames. She was not looking for an antique frame, she was looking for a cheap frame, but since she was looking for an irregular size, she thought she might as well go in and see if maybe there was an inexpensive frame that was a fit for her. She was looking only at the larger ones, not quite poster size but larger than most photograph frames. She whipped out her measuring tape and started measuring.

TURNABOUT IS FAIR PLAY

❖❖❖

They were a family of four, the Dotton family, billionaires and philanthropists. Their philanthropy was not usually for humans, but for animals, there were too many humans that were cruel. They rescued animals when they could and they bought hundreds of thousands of acres to keep them safe. These reserves were in all parts of the country to accommodate any and all animals, and they were well protected. If you wonder how they could protect hundreds of thousands of acres from poachers you need to know one more thing about the family. They were all immensely powerful spiritually. Not like witches and warlocks but more powerful, like sorcerers, enchanters, and mages. If there were areas of sorcery where one fell short, another member of the family was proficient. It worked out well.

The youngest in the family was Ebbie. She was small but mighty, the most powerful one in the family. Like the rest of them, she loved all animals, but she was particularly partial to cats. Her protective nature at times intruded into her social life. Maybe it should be the other way around, her social life sometimes attempted to intrude into her protective nature. Several years ago she was dating a young man who admitted he was not overly fond of animals and especially cats. Ebbie assumed it was because cats are more aloof than dogs and he did not care for their independence.

After a couple of dates she found out that was not the reason at all. She could not trust him around her housecats and she saw him kick one out of the way. He was a world class asshole and evidently a moron who believed the lunacy about cats killing babies by stealing their breath. Ebbie could not abide this caliber of idiot.

Oddly enough, just a few days later he called 911. When they arrived he appeared to be suffocating. In between gasps he said, "a cat is stealing my breath! Find it and get it out." The apartment was locked when he let them in and they searched but found nothing in there with him. The responders could see he was in distress but there was no cat present. They gave him a breathing treatment and suggested he see a therapist. As they left a soft breeze followed them out of the apartment along with a couple cat hairs.

Remember, this was a special family. When they loved, they loved dearly and thoroughly, but when they hated, they could be very wicked, only to the bad guys mind you. Obviously, they could not give homes to all the animals in the shelters but they could help the shelters, and they did. They paid contractors to make the shelters more like homes, with room to run and play, with comfortable bedding, and of course food and toys. Because of the family's donations, these shelters did not have to rely on volunteers. People were paid well to play with animals. This was the best that could be done until all animals had found a loving home but that was not going to happen until breeders stopped breeding and puppy/kitty mills were abolished.

Ebbie and her family visited many breeders and found in some situations they were barely above the conditions of puppy/kitty mills. This did not sit well with the family. A simple binding spell prevented any further births but Ebbie knew that this may not bode well for the animals. She would have to watch them closely to ensure that the animals were not abused in any way. For the greedy breeders, when their money making well had gone dry, they were no longer inclined to feed or house these animals. They were liabilities that were either shot or left to starve. Ebbie stepped in before any of this happened. The animals were saved. She could not abide people who abused animals.

The reputable breeders were treated kind, by the family, compared to the treatment given to owners of animal mills. When they found them, and they always did, the animals were rescued immediately, the owners, maybe not.

The Dottons felt good about their rescue missions but they had to do it area by area. When they touched the lives of every living animal needing rescue in the state they would move to another state. They were very powerful but they had not yet come up with the way to just blink and save every cat, dog, horse, bird, etc. The living animals were saved in this area so now they moved on to the final phase.

This area was very big on hunting. There were big hunt clubs where a person could go to arrange a big game hunt. Canned hunts were the big thing here. Some wealthy guy has a lot of land so he fences it and brings in exotic animals for other wealthy assholes to hunt. Hunt? No, that is not the right word. These animals are fenced in so they have no chance of escaping. It is like killing something exotic in your backyard. Lions were the main attraction for these assholes who called themselves big game hunters. Lions are cats. Ebbie loved cats.

The family had timed this perfectly. There were flyers and advertisements circulating everywhere about the hunters meeting at the Big Game Hunt Club. Hunters and would-be hunters, came from all over to attend the seminar and to see all the animals that were slaughtered. They looked at them in awe. Never once picturing them alive and with family, but just as trophies, taken by the heroic, imposing, hunters.

The day before the big event the family visited the Big Game Hunt Club. Maybe visited is not the right word, the club was closed. The place was huge, four enormous rooms, all full of dead, stuffed animals.

As they walked into the first great room Ebbie's stomach lurched to her throat as her eyes filled with tears. She ran back to the bathroom and barely made it in time to throw up everything in her stomach. Her eyes were spilling along with her breakfast and lunch. She could not unsee what she had seen in one quick second. In the center of that great room stood a pride of lions. Not just one or two, a pride. This awe-inspiring group of magnificent creatures, females around the noble king. Dead. Killed so they could decorate this shithole. On a branch overhead rested the beautiful, sleek, leopard. Also dead. Also killed for later decoration. Majestic creatures all on display in not just one great room but four rooms. One room was not big enough. On the walls also hung the heads of many animals slaughtered needlessly. Ebbie could not linger any longer. She had seen enough. She knew what she had to do.

The family walked around the club shaking their heads. The animals were all posed and some appeared in hunting mode. A smaller exhibit showed an ocelot chasing a mouse, even the mouse was stuffed. As if the rooms were not full enough the walls were all adorned with heads. It was abominable.

Ebbie told them she would handle this with a couple of spells. One for the animals that had been stuffed and one for the animal heads on the walls, the ones who had been beheaded for decoration. For those with no bodies she would create them. She would perform the spells now to become reality the next day when the club was filled with so-called hunters.

She spread her arms and electric shot out of her fingertips and circled and arced around the entire building. She started chanting:

"You should never decorate a bastard's den
I'll make you your old selves again
Back to what you were before this sin

All organs and bones now placed back in
Fur now dull, be returned to life
Teeth restored and sharp as a knife
Feathers once colorful now brittle and dull
All plumage glorious again, better and full
Brain recovered to work as before
Maybe even better, maybe even more
Everything running as good as new
You're totally perfect, a whole new you
I give you youth and forever friends
On us you can continually depend
You will start your shortened life anew
To be free to do what animals do
Magic will transport you to a new home
Independence will give you freedom to roam
First I will see that we get our revenge
For this is a sin that we all must avenge
Somehow we need to show women and men
Trophies are not made of your living skin
So all dead is alive, right down to the mouse
Let these assholes decorate their own fucking house."

Ebbie chanted another spell for those who would need
bodies and the family left.

The next day, late that afternoon, all television
programs were interrupted with breaking news. It
mentioned two hundred guests who had attended the
seminar at the Hunt Club had died but did not give details.
Details were given however to a supermarket magazine.
One witness was the Hunt Club cleaning woman. She was
so frazzled at the scene that she could hardly talk about it,
but she did, oh, did she ever!

She described in detail how all these naked people were
in poses on the displays, much like the animals had been.
There was one where the naked man lying in the middle was
surrounded by naked women, on their hands and knees, all
around him. There was a woman lounging on a suspended

branch with one hand seeming to reach out to those walking by the tree. In another room there were naked people on their hands and knees reaching their heads over a stream to get a drink while there was a naked man in the stream, stretched out and reaching to bite one of those getting a drink. There was a room where most of the naked people were in the trees and the walls were full of human heads. Her descriptions went on and on.

The police were baffled. There was not a drop of blood anywhere and the taxidermy performed on the humans was head and shoulders above (no pun intended) what any local taxidermist could do. This was not a normal crime scene. The police chief remembered hearing about something bizarre like this a few counties over. He looked it up and found very little information available. The only thing he found interesting was that what was once a big hunting community was no longer interested in big game hunting.

The Dottons are working their way across the country. Shame on those who are cruel to animals. They love all animals and Ebbie Dotton is partial to cats.

www.ingramcontent.com/pod-product-compliance
Lightning Source LLC
Chambersburg PA
CBHW071904220626
47052CB00002B/200